Dark Tales of the Inland

Seas Region

by Bob Stevens

ISBN: 978-0-578-56891-1
eISBN: 978-0-578-56964-2

First Printing 2019

23 22 21 20 19   5 4 3 2 1

Dark Tales of the Inland Seas Region
by Bob Stevens

jrefund no. 1 (2019)

Pinus Resinosa

Gretchen was all alone in the laundromat. It was just past midnight, snowing again, and her boyfriend Billy was late.

She thought, if he is not here in less than five minutes, I am just going to curl up on one of these towels and close my eyes.

She yawned.

Her laundry was done.

It had been done for almost half an hour and the damn television hanging up in the corner stared back at her with a useless dark screen. Gretchen could see her warped reflection in that screen: curved and distant. She looked small—a burrowing animal caught by flashlight surprise in her den of roots. And she was dismayed by the way she was hunched over. The reflection revealed a twenty-three-year-old woman who looked much older. When an image of her mother sitting in the same laundromat not so long ago morphed with her own, she shivered and had to look away.

1

It had been a long day. The poor girl had worked the late shift the night before, and today her sister needed someone to watch the kids; but what her sister promised would only take three hours took closer to five because the storm had rolled in and blown everything off schedule. On top of that, Billy had been driving her around everywhere because her stupid, goddamn car was still in the shop. It really wasn't fair to get mad at him for being late. He was so sweet. Especially after all that shuttling in that old truck with all the lake-effect snow that never seemed to let up. He had been a regular angel. And if he needed to stop at the Porcupine Grill and have a couple beers with Jay, well that was his right. He had recently adopted the Winnipeg Jets as his team, and she knew they were playing. Maybe he had gotten caught up in the game.

Gretchen yawned again.

The snow seemed to be falling faster, more aggressively. Visibility was low. Even if he hadn't stopped at the bar, it would still take him a few extra minutes. She wondered why anyone had ever decided to put this damn laundromat out here, so far away from everything else.

Gretchen, out of habit, checked her phone. The battery was still dead.

Oh, Gretch, poor girl, you have had better days, she thought.

Moments later, caught in a thought of Billy with his shirt off in the firelight of his cabin on Ferriday Lake, she saw something moving in the white squall outside. Something with a light brown muzzle. At first, she had the fantastic notion that it was a black bear inexplicably lumbering along on its hind legs through the thickly falling snow, maybe even sleepwalking through visions of a hidden meadow redolent with the languid aroma of blueberries. It must be a confused bear. A confused bear was a dangerous bear. Gretchen blinked, and the image was gone.

You are tired, girl, she told herself. You won't see another bear until April. Maybe it is time to catch a little shut eye. Billy will be here soon...

But an inner voice cautioned against this possible misstep: There is absolutely no one around for miles. When was the last time you saw anybody drive by?

Twenty minutes? Probably more. You are too isolated to curl up and float off to dreamland.

But I'm so tired, and he'll be here any minute, she thought.

She had to stay awake.

Then she saw him, and this time there was no mistaking the figure for a somnambulist bear. It was a large man walking through the snow — a very large man she didn't know. The closer the stranger came to the lunar glow of the parking lot lights, the better she could see him: details Gretchen wished had remained hidden. This was less of a man and more of a beast. It's no wonder she thought he was something less than human at first, because he was well over six feet tall and maybe three hundred pounds. He was thick-bodied and wearing a furry coat. What she had mistaken for a light-brown muzzle was an ice-encrusted beard. He came closer. He saw her looking at him and waved stiffly as if to say, here I am, I'm comin' in. She instinctively fell backwards, away from his advance. Shit, she thought, where the hell is Billy anyway? If he really is watching that damn game at the Porcupine right now, he can forget about…

The door opened and the stranger entered with a dramatic burst of snow and whistling wind.

She gulped.

The chaffed redness of his exposed cheeks and the almost blackened tip of his frostbitten nose suggested he had been out in the elements for quite some time. Now he had found a place to warm up. Now he had found Gretchen. He was wearing snow shoes that, once he shuffled his way inside the laundromat, revealed themselves to be hand-made. The stranger slid them off, big chunks of snow falling from his broad shoulders and from his long curling hair. He coughed.

The frail Gretchen forced a smile.

The man then slid off his heavy backpack. The way he slung it down to the floor demonstrated both a considerable amount of brute strength and frustration. It hit the floor with a heavy thud, and he grunted.

"Fucking brutal out there."

She nodded meekly. "Sure is."

"Fucking brutal…"

She took out her phone again and pretended it was working. She checked an imaginary message and then tucked it away. She realized she wasn't tired anymore. She was wide awake.

"What time is it?" he asked.

Initially, she pretended not to hear him. Then she shrugged. "That clock up there isn't working. Nothing in here but the washers and dryers are working, and even they aren't working that good."

"I mean on your phone. What time is it on your phone?"

She forced another smile that was less convincing than her first. "I didn't notice. Around midnight?"

He whipped off his hat and gave it a good shake. "Could you check?"

"I think it said around midnight…"

"Could you just fucking check?"

Now he was walking over. He wanted to see her phone. Time for honesty.

"The battery just died."

The stranger narrowed his eyes. "Guess we're alone then?"

Gretchen licked her lips. "Yeah, I guess."

He shook his head. "You have no idea who I am, do you?"

"I don't think so."

"I'm Pinus Resinosa."

"Oh."

"I'm the great poet, Pinus Resinosa."

"Oh, I guess I don't know much about poetry. Wish I did, though."

He nodded in grim disapproval. "Figures."

"No, really…"

"See this?"

She shivered as he reached aggressively into his grimy backpack—it glistened with melted snow like some monstrous slug pulled from a bog. When he brought his hand back out, it was holding what seemed to be a journal bound in animal skin. That is *animal* skin, she thought nervously, isn't it?

"See this?" he asked again.

She nodded.

"This is my journal." He scratched his whiskers with bruised and discolored fingernails in a weary appraisal of his work. His arm sagged, as if the

7

journal became heavier. "This is my terrible journal…"

"I see," she said.

"Do you want to know what's in it?"

She paused. "Only if you care to share."

"You wouldn't pry."

"Of course not."

"Well then, if you really want to know the butane glow that ripples over the ridges of my mind then you have to dig into these pages — these scrawled and heartsick pages."

"I see."

The flicker of one of the overhead fluorescents, as mirrored in the parking lot window, gave the staccato impression of headlights coming from out on the road. But it was just an impression. No one was coming. No one was there.

"You want me to read to you from my journal?" he asked.

She took a deep breath. "I guess so — sure. It's not like we really have anything else to do. My laundry is finished."

"You nervous about somethin'?"

"No, sir. Just wondering when my boyfriend is gonna show up. He's late."

Pinus Resinosa smiled. The way he smiled was so foul, she expected him to cough up a cloud of green bottle flies. There was something so inherently vile about him that anything seemed possible. Poor Gretchen had the growing fear she was in the actual presence of a demon. The snow evaporated off him too quickly, suggesting he had an inner heat—one that carried the aroma of a deep inferno at its scented core. The man had been vomited forth by the earth. Maybe, she thought, vomited forth from one of the old copper mines not far from Red Jacket and, from that moment on, cursed to wander the frozen night looking for lost souls to consume.

"You got a boyfriend on the way to pick you up?" He was still smiling.

She forced a smile back.

Pinus Resinosa said, "I bet he is a young and strong man with a stern jawbone and a firearm—always a firearm. Oh, I'm sure he will be here soon. At any moment we will see him pull up through that swirling snow in his four-wheel drive chariot to

9

whisk you off to more intimate interiors. I imagine this would be a nice night to curl up by the fire."

Gretchen nodded. Yes, it would, she thought. But she said nothing. She only nodded.

"So, you are done with your clothes. I am done with my walking. Why don't I read to you from my journal to pass the time a bit?"

Goddammit, she was shaking. She could not stop her knee from shaking.

"You need to relax," Pinus Resinosa smiled again. "I am holding if you want to have a puff or two before I start. It's bogflutter tea—guaranteed to heighten the whole experience for you. Might even calm you down. How about it? You smoke?"

"Oh, sure. But not tonight."

"Your boyfriend don't like it?"

"Oh, he doesn't care…"

"He better care or he's gonna fucking lose you."

She nodded. Her knee was still shaking. "Why don't you go ahead and read a little. I mean, why not?"

"Good, I will. This is from my journal." Pinus Resinosa flipped quite a few pages back, shaking his head. "This is a recent one, from just a couple nights ago. I wrote it in a little cabin on Cauldron Lake. Ever hear of that place?"

She shook her head no.

He shrugged. "Don't surprise me. It's a vanishing lake. It moves around and when it pops up there is always trouble. I hope you never see Cauldron Lake. It would, at the very least, rupture your sanity and turn you bug-eyed and strange forever. Your beauty is too precious for such a fate. Though you would be an enticing lunatic. Anyway, the journal…"

"Yes, please."

Pinus Resinosa, with a beleaguered exhale, let his finger drop on the page. "Dated sometime in February on the frozen shores of Cauldron Lake—in a remote cabin with nine feet of snow that form drifts—big drifts sailing over the rooftop edges in hissing, subzero, dry wind. The arctic moon in the open sky outside is breathtaking—it hangs there all full and frozen. The entire snowbound landscape beneath it glows like the moonscape reflected. It's the coldest night of the year. Wind chill makes it feel forty below out there, and the stars are shining their brightest. The swipe of the Milky Way is clear, and our insignificant place in the persistent glow of its fanning skirts is obvious. It never ceases to fill me with wonder. It's been like that since I was only a sapling, hasn't it? The landscape lies in stunned, nocturnal repose after a big blow, and I perch with pen in hand to wonder. The storm picked up steam over Lake Winnipeg three days ago and then barreled down through Lake Manitou. Good thing I have a radio in this fucking cabin. The spirits of those who have died here are strong. I felt the darkness getting stronger as I approached. Of course, I am well aware of the fucked-up shit that has happened on the shores of this lake. Here lies a litany of atrocities. And I am surely in for a haunted ride before dawn breaks. As I write, I can sense the spirits waking up. They are making their presence known by odd little clicking sounds and a pulsating, acrid odor. They are gearing up to manifest. I will meet them with a glass of whiskey in the firelight. I will swallow up the violence of their tortured passage and make them my own. I am strong enough to bear the heaviest of sorrows. It is what I am made of. It is what I bring. I am a poet."

Gretchen swallowed loudly. "Any minute now."

Pinus Resinosa eyed her in stern reproach of the interruption. "Should I keep reading?"

"Oh, that's all right."

"Don't you want to hear about the ravenous shades I bested? Perhaps we will honeymoon on the shores of Cauldron Lake?"

She gnawed on her bottom lip.

"You don't like my reading?"

"Oh, your reading is fine. That's not it at all…"

"Then what is it?"

Gretchen did not respond. She saw headlights. The headlights of Billy's truck. He pulled up and parked, and there he was getting out and waving at her through the snow. When he saw Pinus Resinosa and the blanched look on Gretchen's face, he knew something was wrong. He decided to retrieve the shotgun he kept behind the front seat. In the laundromat, the poet was reaching in his backpack again. Gretchen screamed.

The Demon Spot

"You don't believe me, do you?"

Justin shrugged and toyed with his coffee cup. "Strange things happen every day, but . . ."

"You don't believe me."

"Well, that isn't necessarily true. I would be more specific than that, David. It's not that I don't believe you're telling me what you saw—not at all— it's just that I question the *interpretation* of what you saw. I mean, seems as if you've jumped quickly to some strange conclusions here. You should be telling Marilyn this. She loves all that ghost hunter stuff." He stopped toying with his cup, picked it up and took a sip. A large truck rumbled by on the street outside and he waited for it to pass before continuing. "Just call me skeptical."

"Fuck it then. Forget I mentioned it," David said.

"No need to get angry. You didn't let me finish my thought." Justin smiled at the young waitress as she passed, and she smiled back. "Yes, I am a skeptic by nature, but that certainly shouldn't suggest that I won't entertain your more fantastic claims—at least for the sake of argument—but it might be more productive and, well, more healthy to stick to a rational approach when trying to find the cause of what you've observed. That's all I'm saying. Okay?"

David was beginning to loathe Justin more and more, but he took a deep breath and, instead of calling him an arrogant dick, which is what he wanted to do, he asked his well-educated breakfast companion to offer some examples of how one might pursue the suggested rational approach.

"Well, first off, you'll need assistance."

I was hoping you'd say that, you predictable fuck, David thought. "Assistance? What kind of assistance?"

Every abandoned building has a story, and the neighborhood where David Hill was living had several to choose from. His apartment was in an imposing, five-story brick structure originally built in 1917 as a hotel and, unlike some of those other properties in surrounding blocks, was fully occupied.

His neighbors were a typical urban mixture of small families and college students. While David didn't fall into either of these camps, he found them all friendly in their way and was generally comforted by their presence.

After a long shift at work, it was good to come back to a place that was buzzing with life, especially in a part of the city whose landmarks included the grim blemishes of vacant lots enclosed by barbed wire fences and vandalized homes abandoned long ago. Spectral clouds rose from open manholes to haunt the empty avenues, but the university was only blocks away and it really wasn't so bad. David liked coming home and hearing the music, chatter, and television sets of his many neighbors, muffled by doorways and given strange harmony by the echo chambers of long hallways.

He was a lonely man, but he never felt completely alone. He knew that if he suddenly fell sick and needed a ride to the hospital, he just had to hobble down the hall and help would be waiting. It was this comfort, combined with the cheap rent, that had kept him living at the Stanfield Apartments for three years. He also enjoyed urban exploration. Almost every Sunday morning he would set out from his place with a shoulder bag, a mug of coffee, and his camera to investigate the ruins of the City of Riverbend.

It was during one of these solitary expeditions, on a cold March day of drifting flurries, that David found something remarkable in an old house on Jarvis Street. The house was missing its front door, a substantial portion of its roof, and most of its window glass. After he ventured through the gray, shadowy rooms of accumulated trash on the first floor, he took a deep breath and decided to turn on his flashlight. He cautiously made his way down the creaking wooden stairs that led into the basement. He was afraid.

There were good reasons to be afraid. The more conspicuous contents of the trash he'd kicked through included ample evidence of recent drug use, and this meant that there was a chance he would encounter a desperate and perhaps dangerous individual lurking in the shadows below. He stomped his feet a few times on the top stairs, then listened for a reaction, but heard nothing save the breezy whistle of subzero air gliding through the house. Stained curls of loose wallpaper strips fluttered uneasily. Some unknown presence seemed to join him at that point, and he shuddered. I'm not alone, he thought, someone or something is in here with me.

In spite of these unsettling impressions, he carefully made his way down. The cracked and warped steps, as he expected, groaned and creaked under his weight. Fearing they would break, and dreading the possibility of a bad fall, he made his way along with great caution. In the center of the basement there was a curious, bricked column that resembled a chimney in size and appearance. Covered in graffiti and surrounded by empty liquor bottles, spent hypodermic needles, and newspaper shreds, it didn't seem to serve any structural or aesthetic purpose. The idea that it was built to hide something immediately popped into his mind as he scanned its length slowly with the beam of his flashlight. He wondered why no one, either in the spirit of curiosity or mindless destruction, had ever knocked it down. Noises from upstairs that couldn't be attributed to the winter breeze prompted him to cut his first visit to the basement on Jarvis Street short, but he returned in the frozen weeks that followed. It was only a matter of time before he brought a pickaxe and sledgehammer to discover what was inside.

"Well, by assistance I mean . . ." Justin was uncharacteristically struggling to find the right words.

"You mean I should have someone help me with my little experiments. Maybe they're not scientific enough?"

"Well, not necessarily. I'm just saying that maybe you should have someone else come along. Seems like that house is in a sketchy neighborhood anyway. Maybe you shouldn't be going there alone."

"I do this shit all the time. It's fine."

Justin sighed, then said, "Yeah, but it would be good to have someone come along with you just to corroborate what you see. Maybe even film it. It would be a lot more convincing from where I'm sitting if I could see some evidence. All I have to go on is what you're telling me and, like I said, it's not that I think you're lying to me, it's just that, well, it's a bit far-fetched. Do you know anyone at the university?"

"Like scientists?"

"Not necessarily, but just . . ."

David pretended to think for a moment, fished out his pack of cigarettes, then shook his head. "Seems like it was a mistake even bringing it up to you, but whatever."

"It depends on how you phrase things. It depends on your approach. What I would do is keep your supernatural ideas to yourself and imply that you are convinced that there is some rational explanation and you'd just like some help figuring it out. Or maybe you could take the health hazard angle. That's practical, and no one would think you're crazy for being concerned about animals dying, right?"

"That's all, huh?" David lit his cigarette, exhaled a plume of grey smoke, then reclined his large body into the booth. "I imagine you have a rational explanation handy?"

"Well, from what you've told me thus far, I'd say that there must be something poisonous in the air, something noxious. Have you kept any of the dead animals?" Justin asked.

"Hell no, my apartment smells bad enough as it is. Why?"

"I was just thinking that another thing you might want to do is to take one of the carcasses somewhere—maybe the Humane Society—and see if they can determine the cause of death."

"You want me to take a dead rat to the Humane Society?"

"No, I guess not a rat, but—"

"Listen, Justin, it's not noxious fumes." David took a deep drag off his cigarette. "I've got a pretty good sense of smell, and I think I'd pick up on a deadly gas in the air. Besides, don't you think I'd get sick too? Just from being in that basement? You're just gonna hafta admit that you don't have an explanation for it."

"Just because I can't explain it doesn't mean that you're right," said Justin.

"Come see for yourself. I happen to have a cage of mice in the car right outside. I was planning to go there today anyway."

"I don't think so."

"You're afraid," David said.

Justin smiled, but a new redness in his face meant that David had hit his mark. "While I might be afraid of some abandoned building in an urban slum, I'm most certainly not afraid of some imagined demonic presence residing in a basement there."

"Maybe Marilyn would go with me."

"No, she will not."

"You said it yourself. She loves this kinda stuff. Can I ask her?"

"No."

"Really? I didn't realize she needed your permission to—"

"Alright, fine, *I'll* go," said Justin.

"Morning is the safest time. How about now?"

Justin responded by finishing his coffee in an angry slurp, sliding out of his seat, and walking towards the door. David followed, and soon they were on their way to visit the demon spot.

Most people will tell you that they would quietly celebrate the unexpected death of any number of undesirable folks, but those who would tell you with conviction that they would do the killing themselves—if they thought they could get away with it—are another breed entirely. David Hill, the bespectacled and slightly obese subject of this little tale, was a particularly interesting and tragic example of this second breed. Although he certainly wasn't inherently evil and, on the contrary, was regarded by most as an unerringly polite, endearingly shy and admirably generous young man, he was sadly undone like so many before him by an unhealthy obsession with an unrequited love. Her name was Marilyn Milanovic, and she was a disastrous choice for a man of his reserved nature and mediocrity. He simply wasn't her type. Even though David and Marilyn had grown up together as neighbors, they were certainly not equals. She blossomed into an exotic flower whose fragrant brunette energy attracted all manner of amorous attention. All the while, David languished behind her, struggling in high school and struggling in college, suffering the cruel dishonor of a persistent virginity. Perhaps it would've been better if she could've summoned the cruelty to abandon their increasingly awkward friendship completely, but Marilyn always erred on the side of compassion and insisted on keeping in touch.

In the spirit of her endearing optimism, she often arranged for David to meet and date women that she knew, but nothing ever worked out. The dull pain of these failures was made even more unbearable by the ease with which she tended to her own romantic endeavors. Marilyn had her choice of men and, conscious of her numerous attributes, was understandably drawn to ambitious, talented, intelligent, and handsome types. Eventually, she found her match, and after an exciting and well-traveled two-year courtship, he proposed and she accepted. His name was Justin Cavella and, like her, was both a svelte charmer and a talented architect. They were an impressive couple who inspired luminous accolades from everyone but the predictable and disdainful few whose own lack of happiness perpetually hinders their ability to appreciate it in others. They established themselves in the city, and it didn't take them long to find a stunning late Victorian house which was coincidentally less than ten miles from the neighborhood where long-suffering college dropout David Hill was renting a one-bedroom apartment.

"That's our little house of evil," David said as he pulled up to the curb and parked. "You sure you want to go through with this?"

Justin was visibly bothered by the sight of the place. A group of clouds had thickened above and seemed to be on the edge of raining. "You feel safe leaving your car parked here?"

"This piece of shit? Nobody wants to steal a junker like this, besides, crime doesn't seem to be a problem around here this early in the morning. I've done it before. Don't worry." David reached into the backseat, grabbed his flashlight and a tiny cage with six squeaking mice inside, then opened the door. "Come on, let's go."

Justin followed, and the two of them walked

across the tall weeds of the front yard. Somewhere nearby, a dog started barking loudly. David didn't seem too worried about the dog, wherever it was, and responded to its still invisible approach by swinging his little cage of mice and whistling. Once they were over the threshold, which no longer presented the nuisance of a door, Justin felt a powerful chill spread across his lower back. He wasn't sure if his finer senses had kicked in and actually detected a change in the atmosphere, or if it was merely the unwelcome symptom of ingesting too much supernatural nonsense with his breakfast. Justin decided not to mention this odd sensation to his guide. At the top of the stairs, David paused to light another cigarette with an unnecessary and deliberate slowness.

"You really sure you want to see this?" David asked as he waved out the match.

"Yes, of course, I've come this far," Justin said, realizing with a touch of embarrassment that he was whispering unnecessarily. "Really, I want to see this but . . ."

"But what?"

"Well, to be perfectly honest, I'm a little concerned about that dog outside."

"It's a hazard of the hobby but trust me, it's really not a problem." He patted the front pocket of his trousers, cigarette bobbing on his lower lip. "It's called pepper spray. Works on people too."

Justin felt a sudden and urgent need to urinate, so David obligingly smoked and waited while his companion relieved himself in a corner where wall stains indicated he was merely the most recent in a long line of pissers that had come before. It was a singular moment. The refined architect emptying his bladder while the grimy slacker looked on. They certainly did make a very odd couple, but Marilyn had told her new husband that it was important to her—however strained the effort might be at first—that the two most important men in her life get to know and appreciate one another. The request was met with a gracious response. To say that Justin had gone out of his way to fulfill the wishes of his wife was, by any reasonable measure, an understatement. He had taken David out for drinks, to a hockey game, and now he was acting against his better judgment to indulge this misguided fool in a potentially perilous exploit into a dangerous neighborhood. I love you, Marilyn, I do this because I love you, Justin thought as he zipped up, but this is clearly miles above and beyond the call of duty.

"Okay." Justin forced a smile. "Are we ready to descend?"

"Shhh, listen."

Justin strained his ears but heard nothing. "What?"

"The dog stopped barking. Dogs are afraid of this place." David smiled, and it wasn't forced. "Follow me."

With the help of the flashlight, they carefully went down the stairs. As if sensing the fate that awaited them, the mice in David's cage started to frantically scurry and rage against their confinement. Seeing even the tiniest creatures struggle nauseated Justin, and he tried to block out their piteous screeching. It was useless, and he felt his stomach twist into cramping knots. Justin thought, this is distasteful and cruel and hideous and wrong . . .

"There it is." David said, training the flashlight

beam on a spot in the middle of the floor. With its collection of bones and tiny corpses, it resembled a sacrificial altar. Another cage nearly identical to the one David was holding was sitting there as well, filled with dead and decomposing mice. "That's the demon spot. Whatever living creature passes through that spot goes crazy for a few seconds, almost as if they're on fire, and then they fall still, dead as a doorknob. The day I knocked down the bricks, I felt this evil breeze wash over me. I swear to God I saw these images, these laughing red faces with bloody teeth all crackling with flame. I fell down on the ground right here and almost passed out. When I got back up, I found a little pile of bones inside, mostly rat bones. I'm not sure how they got in there, or if whoever walled the spot up was just too impatient or scared to clean away the little corpses but . . ."

"But what?" asked Justin.

"Everything I put in there dies."

Justin decided not to give his guide the satisfaction of visible fear. He stayed calm. "I suppose you were the one who drew the chalk outline around it?"

"Yeah, just to remind myself."

"Have you ever stepped inside?"

"Hell no. Why risk it? I wouldn't even want to stick a hand in there." He plucked the cigarette from his mouth with the hand that held the flashlight, exhaled a cloud of smoke, then sniffed. "Can you smell anything out of the ordinary?"

Justin sniffed too. "No, I guess nothing but . . . decay."

"No pungent gasses?"

Justin shook his head.

"Well, then, how do you explain this?" He placed the mouse cage down in a reverential manner that reminded Justin of devout Hindus that he'd once seen making offerings at a temple near Calcutta. The name of the temple escaped him, and he had no time to waste trying to remember it because David was nudging the cage across the dirty floor, slowly towards the ominous chalk boundary with the tip of his boot. Unfortunately, the steady jostling of his prodding popped the latch on the door, which was apparently not fastened properly. The frightened mice sensed their shot at freedom and poured out like water, scattering to the safety of dark corners of the basement. David cursed, tossed away his cigarette, fell to his knees, and fumbled around desperately, but the last mouse had already located the exit and pounced away before he could intervene. "Fuck! This stupid fucking cage, piece of fucking shit."

Justin exhaled, glad the mice had found a way to liberate themselves. He hoped the whole episode had played itself out. "Well, that was convenient."

David glared at him. "What's that supposed to mean?"

"Nothing. Maybe we'll try again some other time, but now I think we should probably go. Marilyn is expecting me back within the hour." He glanced down at his watch and nodded. "Yeah, I'm cutting it close as it is. Sorry, Dave. Oh, but she wanted me to tell you that you're invited over for dinner later if you can make it."

David stood up, holding his faulty cage like a weapon. "I don't need you being all condescending. You think I planned for those mice to get out?"

"I'm sure you didn't."

"You still don't believe me, do you?"

"David, be reasonable. Why would I? Even if you'd managed to slide those poor caged mice into your little evil square and they died mysteriously, I would still seek a more rational explanation than the one you seem to have settled with. Now, really, I don't feel comfortable here and I would appreciate it if we could leave."

"You say you don't believe me, but you're scared."

"Really?"

"You know there's a demonic presence down here," said David.

"No, actually I'm pretty convinced that the opposite is true."

"Then go stand in there. I dare you."

Justin felt his fear subsiding and his senses returning. "Shouldn't you be concerned that I might die? Now you're hurting my feelings here."

"I'd save you."

"Why don't you stand in there instead and let me be the one who does any necessary saving?" asked Justin.

"I'd never stand in there—no fucking way. And you know what? I don't give a shit what you think, because I'm personally convinced, without a doubt, that a demon is stuck there, probably bound by a spell. I also know that whatever crosses into his little prison gets destroyed by it."

"David, really, listen to yourself."

"You go in there then and see what happens."

Justin was the kind of a man who had a very hard time resisting a challenge, and David knew it. He could see Justin progressing from incredulous to annoyed. He could also see him bolstering his courage and knew, at that moment, that Justin had taken the bait. David felt a dreamlike haze pass over him when he realized that his plans, stage by stage, had transpired almost exactly as he had imagined them. Could it really be this easy? He had to stop himself from smiling, especially when he heard the following.

"Okay, fine, I'll stand on your demonic spot, but then we're leaving, okay?"

All David could do was watch, almost salivating with eager anticipation, as Justin walked over and, without hesitation, stepped inside.

Several hours later, as the afternoon started to wind down, David was sitting in his apartment drinking beer — radio off, despondent. It was raining in a steady and dreary fashion which only added to the gloom of his thoughts. He'd been drinking ever since he returned home, and when he finished his ninth bottle, he rose to use the bathroom only to feel his head roll and sputter like a carousel taking on water. He hadn't eaten since breakfast. He was drunk. With all the concentration he could muster, he made it to the toilet, pissed, then lingered above the sink to stare at the sad wreck of his reflection.

He couldn't understand why the goddamn demon spot hadn't worked. How could that motherfucker still be alive after standing there for so long? David closed his eyes and brought back the image of Justin boldly stepping into the chalk square, crunching with a little grimace on the animal bones gathered there. Then he waited and breathed deeply and waited and shifted his weight and waited and scratched the back of his neck and waited. Finally

Justin delivered the insult of all insults, faking a big yawn and asking calmly for permission to end the little experiment. How did he do it? Had the malignant energies, so potent when the bricks first came down, all been diluted and dispersed? Did humans have some immunity to whatever was there?

David opened his eyes and found a murderer looking back at him in the streaked and spotted bathroom mirror. Even though his attempt hadn't been successful, he now knew, and would always know, that he was capable of not only killing someone, but of relishing it as well. He remembered the almost giddy rush of exhilaration that swept through him when Justin agreed to test the demon spot. He remembered hoping that death wouldn't come quickly. He had hoped for a painful struggle. He had wanted to see his unknowing adversary stiffen in anguish and gasp for air. You are a fucking monster, he said to his reflection, and then he let his face drop. The boozy tears that followed fell with little splashes into the sink and ran down the drain.

It was exactly eleven minutes before midnight

when he heard the phone ringing through the heavy, wet curtains of his slumbering stupor. He was sprawled on his couch, completely naked, and it took several rings before a basic understanding of his surroundings began to return to him. He was still in his apartment. He had been drinking most of the day. It was night. He had smoked too many cigarettes. The phone was ringing. Better pick it up.

"Hello?"

"David?"

"Yeah, it's me."

"David Hill?"

"Yeah, who is this?"

"It's Justin."

"Oh." David felt his head throb with the refreshed memory of his failure. He used a weary right hand to rub the soreness of his temples. "What's up?"

"You never came over for dinner."

"I fell asleep."

"Well, we waited almost two hours, then ate without you."

"You sound funny."

"Too much wine. Sounds like you've been drinking a little too."

"So what?"

"Listen, I did not mean to be dismissive or demeaning earlier today. Sometimes, when I'm a little stressed or annoyed, I can behave badly. My apologies."

"Did Marilyn force you to call?" asked David.

"No, well—she didn't exactly force me, but she did suggest it." He took an audible sip of something, presumably wine. "We were worried when you didn't show up, and we called you about half an hour ago. You didn't answer."

"Thanks, really. Now that you know I'm safe, can I get back to sleep?"

"Sleep? It's still early!"

"What time is it?"

"It's not even midnight. We really want you to come over." Justin cupped the phone to talk to someone, but David couldn't hear what it was about. "Marilyn insists that you come over. If you don't feel safe driving, then we'll get you a cab. If you stick around here for one cocktail too many and want to stay the night, that would be fine. We have the guest room all made up. Please, David, just come over for a drink or two."

"Why?"

"If you keep asking me questions, you'll make me ruin the surprise. Marilyn is a little angry with me as it is. You'll be doing me a big favor. Come on."

David couldn't help but be amused with this offer. The man he'd tried to kill earlier in the day was now insisting that he come over for drinks. While he really didn't want to see Justin again, he could never pass up a chance to see Marilyn. David would have to take a shower and shave. "Give me half an hour."

"Thanks. We'll be waiting."

"Whatever." David hung up.

Even after a cold shower, he couldn't shake the groggy suspicion that something was terribly wrong.

David decided to drive himself. He'd been to their house twice before, and had no problem finding it again. When he parked curbside, he saw lights on downstairs in the parlor, and in one of the bedrooms on the second floor. The rain had stopped, and a full moon, large and almost lavender, emerged to put a lambent touch on every drenched surface and reflecting puddle. David stepped out of his car and paused in the street to finish his cigarette. The neighborhood was a respectable one, and he could feel the weight of its dignity in the immense hush that stretched all the way down the block. Big houses slumber deeply. Big houses guard their secrets. He wondered if urban decay would ever find its way all the way to this neighborhood. One day, would the families flee and the vandals enter? Would weather be allowed to work unchecked on the rooftops and the lawns? Would these exclusive addresses one day be anyone's to explore and excavate? He hoped so.

David crushed out his cigarette on the wet street, walked up to the front door, pressed the doorbell, and heard the muffled sound of its mellow chimes reverberating inside. He waited for half a minute before ringing again, then repeated the procedure for a third and fourth time. Feeling uncomfortable on the porch of such an imposing home—which clearly did not belong to him—he twisted the doorknob with impatience. After a soft click, the heavy door fell open.

"Hello?" His voice echoed. He stepped inside and shut the door behind him. "Hello?"

In a very short period of time, Justin and Marilyn had really decorated the place nicely. David's footfalls were muted by a long, heavy rug as he made his way down the hall that ran past the staircase and towards the kitchen. He could see a soft light glowing back there, and even though it was a logical place for a couple to be have drinks, David found it empty. The old nineteenth-century house sat so still in the witching hour, that with the full moon hanging outside, it made David think of ghosts. He could almost hear them emerging from the walls upstairs, hooting softly like owls, but just as he was starting to get a little frightened, he heard Justin calling from the basement.

"David? Is that you?"

"Yeah." David walked over to the top of the stairs. "Want me to come down?"

"Please."

He was still feeling the effects of a long day of drinking. David nearly lost his footing, and it forced him to grab the railing. The steps were slippery. He glanced at his feet. The steps were actually wet. He took another cautious step, but couldn't prevent his heel from skidding and he fell, thudding his way loudly down to the cellar floor where he landed painfully on his side. He knew he was hurt. When he held his hand up to his face, he found it covered in blood.

"Don't worry, friend, it's not your blood." Justin was standing over him, shirtless and glistening with gore. "The first time I stabbed her was at the top of the stairs there. Then I stabbed her all the way down. Very fucking messy. Arterial blood, you know."

David stared at the blood. "Jesus Christ."

"Yes, I suppose that's an accurate comparison. She bled as much as Jesus Christ but—in a display of my more tender impulses and in spite of my, shall we say, altered condition—she did not have to suffer as long as the Son of God." Justin paused to look in strange wonder at his crimson hand and the long knife that it held. "Dreadful."

David tried to stand, but the sharp pain in his ankle caused him to fall back, wincing.

"Oh, you're hurt. Here, let me help." Justin bent down and extended a hand, but when David reached out to grab it, he instead received the slash of a knife across his palm.

What followed wasn't a scream, but a series of gasping attempts to scream and a few choked words. "Please . . . Don't . . ."

Justin pretended to consider the pleading, then lunged forward and swiped a gash into David's forehead. He stepped back, wiped the blade on his pants, and shook his head slowly. "You and your fucking demon spot. Look."

He walked back behind the old furnace, bent down, and picked up a severed arm. He threw it at David. "You know who that belongs to?"

The arm landed on the floor just a few feet from him. David wiped away the blood that ran into his eyes and found that it was mixing with new tears.

"If you can't guess, maybe this will help." Justin picked up something else, hefted it into his hands, assumed the stance of a bowler, then rolled the severed head of Marilyn towards him. It flopped and gurgled in a tangle of dark, matted hair. Even though he tried to scurry out of the way, it came to an open-mouthed rest near his feet, her empty eyes staring into his. David kicked at it and made a desperate attempt to crawl back up the slippery steps, but his pursuer calmly followed. An image of the basement in the house on Jarvis Street flashed into David's brain. He felt the knife thump twice into his back. This is where you will die, he thought, as Justin grabbed his ankles and dragged him back behind the furnace, mumbling incoherently.

The Three Voices of the Imp

The Imp watched while sections of his arboreal terrain were cleared for houses and farms but, unlike many of his other elemental spirit kin, he was never scared away by the commotion. He never went to haunt deeper and more private stands of trees to the north. Some of the old woodsy spirits, as you may have read, find humans to be fascinating. They linger where people settle. They sit in the shifting obscurity of wilder vegetation and observe our irrational behavior patterns. They marvel as we buckle under the complex burden of our uniquely human emotions. They get interested. Then they meddle and manipulate, and drive mortals crazy with their folly.

This particular imp is most often spied either by the abandoned, crumbling stone well—where the old water bucket lies spider-webbed and worm-eaten in its depths—or down the trail further, by that towering shagbark hickory. The Imp watches the woods. He always has. He enjoys the company of the

44

squirrels. He spooks the chipmunks into zipping retreat. He grins at all the birds who call the region home but, thorny bastard that he is, never hesitates to play tricks on those just migrating through. The Imp, you see, is very territorial. The Van Horns', slow to wisdom, came to the delayed conclusion that their crackpot ancestors should never have built a house this close to *his* section of the woods.

There has been some general consensus regarding the Imp's physical appearance. He is said to be about four feet tall with a dull, grayish skin color and is usually quite naked; his exposed body is very slender and tightly muscled. He is a quick leaper and climber. Many, in fact, have only caught peripheral glimpses of him and then, upon turning, find him vanished and gone. Other common attributes given to the Imp are a curling, mossy beard and a triangulated stub tail. He is also unfailingly described as having a wavering transparent quality. At times, he can be distinctly visible in every detail, utterly tangible, and then, the next moment, he has morphed into his surroundings, sometimes shrinking back into a rustle of windy leaves or dispersing like blown smoke into every direction—poof! The Imp successfully employs this talent for theatrical effect and is quite good at making memorable entrances and exits. This dramatic flair is the result of watching several long centuries of human reactions and, like any devoted dramatist, the clever Imp has diligently devised what moves an audience so that he may, in turn, summon such reactions as needed via his own manipulations.

His greatest manipulative asset is his voice. The Imp is notoriously loquacious. Accounts of what his magpie orations sound like vary wildly, but when considering them in totality, three common types emerge. The first of these is the softest little whisper by which he weaves blandishments and pleasant revelations which are enticing, relaxing, and sometimes even seductive. He can form a sibilant and altogether pleasant and soft hissing that makes a person feel warm and enchanted. They say he can be downright irresistible when employing such palaver, but he has, unfortunately, two other voices as well. The second one is a rather virile and aggressive kind of masculine speech, which he uses to boast of his prowess in all manner of things while encouraging others to recklessly boast of their own. This voice of the Imp is the voice of a dangerously impatient and persuasive asshole. He can be a bit bawdy when employing this way of speaking, and often quite funny. The third voice, however, is the one dreaded far above the others. Only a tragic few have heard it. It is the voice of apeshit madness. The voice that imparts the inconceivable. The voice that stirs the mind into perpetual vertigo. It is cloying, guttural, hoarse, and gurgling, but it has never ever been described by anyone who still had their sanity intact. I believe you will gain valuable insights into the nature of the Imp if provided with an example of how his nefarious use of each of these three voices has adversely affected Van Horn family history.

The first type of voice was the one Stephen Van Horn spent his whole misspent life hearing. The historic house on the edge of the woods is still known as the Van Horn House. The family lived there for generations. Tragic Stephen was a rare Van Horn in that he had strong artistic sensibilities as opposed to business sense. His was a gentler constitution of pale fragility which only grew worse under the seductive influences of that pesky Imp. The signs came early. It seems as if the boy was attracted to the woods even as an infant. He would caterwaul and cry, and the only way to curtail these fits was to hold him aloft so that he could see the trees. Amusement would sparkle in his tiny eyes and he would smile so sweet, responding to something that no one else could see. The Imp, it should be noted, prefers to make himself visible only to select individuals. So when his mother faced her child to the woods and the crying stopped, she would scan the edge of the forest and see nothing but a confusion of brisk northern breezes rippling the green in random patterns. Was he smiling at the birds? No, said a grave father, the child is seeing that mischievous Imp!

The father's suspicions were confirmed one cloudy late summer afternoon when there was a rare case of a mass sighting. Both parents and a visiting Uncle noticed that the six-year-old Stephen had wandered off while the three adults were absorbed in a heated debate of the political variety. When they went searching for him, their attentions naturally focused on the haunted woodlands and the rudimentary trail that ran through them to the well. They tore down that path, calling his name. The child had managed to wander all the way to the end and, horror of horrors, was seen propped like a ventriloquist's dummy in the lap of that grinning Imp. The awful creature was whispering to him, and little Stephen was laughing. When the adults arrived, the creature set the boy down and then scrambled all double-jointed and spider-like to vanish into the well. It was horrible.

Stephen Van Horn, like others before and after him, had been marked. He was doomed to a lifetime of odd behavior. Those child-like whisperings of the Imp, which he continued to hear until his final day, were said to be the cause of his degeneration into a disastrously devoted poet. His humorless fixations with the varieties of human tragedy and all things sorrowful made him unbearable to be around when he was a young man, and his forays into the real world were, as can be expected, uniformly unsuccessful. What made things worse was that his poetry and his brooding essays did not generate much interest when he presented them to the world. Some of his writing still exists. It is, in all honesty, not very good. This was the true cruelty of the Imp. He provided Stephen with a rampage of creative desires but did not think to give him talent. It's true. His heightened sensitivities and eccentric behavior did not even provide the consolation of great art.

It was this first voice of the Imp — the sibilant and altogether pleasing one — which caused both Stephen Van Horn and my lost wife to fall in love with an idealized nature and daydream their days away. Eventually, Stephen's frustrations with the cruel world he encountered drove him to make two failed suicide attempts. After the second one, a botched hanging, he was institutionalized. After only a year of close observation, he was deemed harmless and allowed to return home to live out his remaining days as a bearded recluse writing saccharine verse and gloomily tending the garden and the flowers. He was often seen sitting on that well, sometimes reading and sometimes talking out loud to no one. He never married, never traveled far, and died at the age of sixty-two in the room above the kitchen. Quite sad.

That was why the Van Horns became so protective of their children. Can you blame them? There was a terrible fear that one day, they themselves would run down that trail and find their own child in the lap of the conniving Imp. They kept their small ones close, and never let them wander near the woods. But when children reach a certain age their wandering, unless one resorts to the questionable use of actual restraints, they can no longer be curtailed. They turn into teenagers and attain both the strong desire and ability to escape. Much of this wanderlust comes from the desperate need for sexual release. Remote or hidden locations become important. Thus, the privacy of the woods beckoned, and it was just this type of irresistible drive that drew the seventeen-year-old Douglas Van Horn into his initial encounter with the Imp.

With hickory nuts crunching underfoot, Douglas was wandering one day in the Imp's domain, preoccupied by feverish thoughts of the female form. He heard a sound in the branches. Something was leaping from tree to tree in the farther reaches of the canopy. As the leaping beastie approached, the rustling and cracking became louder. Douglas instinctively patted his pockets in search of some protection, but he had left his penknife behind in a sequestered cigar box (which, by the way, contained the additional contraband of tobacco and French postcards). The young man was unarmed! He searched the ground for a fallen branch sturdy enough for battle, but before he could find one of suitable thickness, the commotion stopped. Issuing from the shagbark hickory directly overhead, Douglas Van Horn heard that second voice of the Imp. It was virile, aggressive, bawdy, and persuasive.

It was the voice Douglas detected wafting through the breezy afternoon. "I can show you where to find the labial flowers you seek," it said, "and I can nurture you into a nocturnal gardener capable of summoning a wide range of warm bloomings that will make you quite popular once word gets around. Ladies talk," it continued, "and they have a discourse that remains forever fugitive from their husbands."

The Imp said a lot of things like this and, not surprisingly, Douglas began escaping to those woods as often as he could—usually with the tobacco, French postcards, and penknife he forgot the first time—to sit under that big tree and listen for the phantom verbalizations of his salacious instructor. He kept a notebook, but it has long been lost, most likely destroyed in the wake of his scandalous demise. Much of the story, however, survives in great detail. His family culled it directly from the pages and passed it on as part of their oral tradition. According to this vanished document, Douglas did not even see the Imp for the longest time. He only heard that voice. In fact, the creature did not reveal himself to the young man until long after he'd become the most notorious philanderer in the county.

Douglas Van Horn, it seems, fucked his way into nearly every household before a jealous husband finally caught up with him in those enchanted woods and blasted the back of his skull out with a single, well-placed rifle shot. Crows scattered. Gathered deer went leaping away. The boy was only twenty-three at the time. That Imp, monstrous influencer, had turned him into an insatiable and ambitious cad. It brought much shame to the Van Horn house and property.

Many of the women he conquered were taken right back there in those woods. Some say you can still hear their cries and moans when the summer nights hang thick and heavy. The damp perfume of female arousal plays on the breezes. The leaves shiver. Some hauntings, as you may know, are much more distracting than others. Poor Douglas.

The Imp inspires different kinds of madness. He can tilt an individual towards the morose, or sway him just as quickly to the lascivious if he so chooses. But he can also use that third voice and drive a man right out of his wits and directly into raving lunacy. This is what happened to Wilbur Van Horn. Wilbur, whose portrait still hangs in the parlor, was a member of the last generation of Van Horns to reside on the property. What made his unraveling even more lamentable was the fact that he actually did quite well for himself early in life. He excelled in his studies and graduated from every level with honors. His focus became finance, and his attributes included a steel trap mind. He could, for instance, after seemingly cursory glances into the morning's business paper, rattle off how every stock was trading. He was given respect beyond his years. He anticipated trends. He made money. Relatives hailed him as the financial genius who would carry the Van Horn family to new, lucrative heights. He quickly found a job down in Putorious after finishing his graduate work, and was doing quite well for himself until he returned home for a week-long summer vacation.

It was there—while he puffed a steam engine trail of cigar smoke on an early morning stroll through the misty pines back by that well—that he came around to a break in the trees and saw the Imp blocking his path, with the unfurling fern of an aroused cock in hand. The cigar fell out of Wilbur's mouth to sizzle in the dew below. He blinked and blinked but the repulsive image would not go away. Hallucinations, he thought, I have lost my goddamn mind. Then the Imp started speaking. Crazy talk. Talk about how the bristle of the naked berry can slice the purple sap from the center of the mind if you wield such a weapon fearlessly. Talk about the soil-deep navigations of luminous red snakes that lead to spontaneous fires in the thoughts of those who pass above. Talk about the similar permafrost vapors that rise pungent as a dinge fork from burial pits teeming with translucent vipers. Talk that went on and on. Incessant and nonsensical. He put his fingers in his ears and shut his eyes, but still the voice of the Imp came through. He fell to the ground. He tried to scream but nothing came out. Five hours later he wandered back from the woods all muddy and disheveled, much to the horror of his terrified parents and younger sister.

He told them he had gotten lost. He told them he needed to lie down. They carried Wilbur up to his old room and secured him safely under the covers. Should we call a doctor? Were you bit by anything? Wilbur? He didn't answer any of these questions because he had already drifted off. Then he slept fitfully and feverishly for thirteen long hours, and just as his mother was dialing the number of the family physician, he suddenly awoke. After staring around at his surroundings for a few tense moments, his face twisted into a lupine grin and he began laughing uncontrollably.

He threw his covers off and ran out of the

house in a dash, straight into the woods, shedding his clothes along the way. The Imp was calling him back. His family eventually tracked him down a few hours later. He had smeared himself with dirt, and was curled up like a wounded fawn, nibbling in the tufted grasses of a forest clearing. They were able to coax him all the way back to the house as he babbled about ludicrous things like the lord of the brook trout and the sandy etchings in the dust of dead clouds that foretell the fearsome rising of the ants. But Wilbur had some extended moments of clarity as well. He was able to tell them tearfully how the Imp bewitched him. If he calls me then I must come, he said, so strap me down before the moon rises, because that little monster surely has grievous plans for me this evening. But they did not bind him strong enough, and that very night he leapt right through the glass of his bedroom window with a frightening and bloody crash. He ran off like a beast on all fours, bleeding badly. This time the Van Horns called the authorities. They were too frightened to search the dark woods for him on their own. His mother wept uncontrollably in the kitchen while police took their search into the tangles and brambles with flashlights panning. It started to rain. The search went on for over an hour before someone thought to cast their flashlight beam into the vine-covered throat of the old well. Wilbur was down there. His bones were broken and he had bled out. No one saw the Imp, but it can safely be assumed he was admiring his cruel handiwork from a vantage point nearby.

The Lost Mahogany Runabout

This was the foggy cold-water drift Gary had been waiting for—what he had dreamt of so often with his head rested on those soft-blue hospital pillows, lying on his back and watching the snow come down outside while they prodded him for another blood draw. It had been a long winter of hospital stays and one test after another. Now here he was—back in his father's old mahogany runabout with the motor puttering and a spooling wake fanning behind him, invisible in the fog. The wet air was cool on his face and he was shivering despite layers of wool, flannel, and rain gear. April had finally warmed enough for nearly all the snow to melt, but the water maintained a deep and powerful chill. The occasional misting rain that hissed through the ever-shifting clouds came down with a bite. Yet there was an irrefutable freshness to everything. There was a smile on Gary's face. He had the boat back on the water. Not just any boat: his father's boat. His grandfather's boat.

His brother-in-law had done a fine job taking care of her while he was away. Maybe he wasn't so bad after all. He had proven to be a good father, a hard worker, and a passable mechanic. Just listen to that motor. It was a twenty-foot custom runabout meticulously constructed by many calloused hands in the original factory way down below the south side of Lake Beyond in Pointe de Chene. Gary's grandfather bought the boat after returning from the war, and no one had spent more time at the helm of the runabout than him. His memory always hovered close when it was out on the water. The old man was solid as a walnut. Gary's father had grown equally stoic and immovable — traits and affinities which, along with the boat and the family house, became Gary's inheritance. He closed his eyes against the mist as he let the boat glide and let his mind wander. He imagined his grandfather there with him. Then, his mind darkened this vision with the blue complexion of a strangled corpse.

It had been a murder most foul. He opened his eyes and the big billows of fog were still there. He took a deep breath and smelled the rich aroma of the freshly melted marshes. He was in very shallow water and drifting too close to the nearest shore when he felt the whole boat drag in the weeds. It took all the care he could muster to guide the old runabout back to safer water without getting irrevocably snagged. But it was a struggle because his thoughts kept circulating in slurping muddles. He was somehow bewitched by this misty morning. Everything seemed to wobble unsteadily on the edge of consciousness, and the soft purr of the engine would become beaded in the glossy pearls of freshly formed dew. Down he would fall to the very edge of dreaming, but then the spell would pass and he would be alert once more—hands on the banjo wheel, shrouded in prevailing fog. He gathered himself. He knew where he was. He was moving back to the deeper part of the channel.

It was hard to estimate just how many times he had taken this very boat down this very channel, but a conservative guess would be somewhere around fifty. He had not lost his bearings in the fog one bit. When allowed to focus and squint, he recognized every shoal and weedy bend. This was dead reckoning. This was ghosting. The runabout seemed to be guiding itself. It was a fine boat. Not all mahogany but mostly — with cedar for the bottom planking and the planking hulls. The planking hulls were the same chestnut-brown color of his wife's hair before it turned gray. Gary worked his hands on that wheel and thought about her.

He thought about the way she stood in the kitchen when she was lathering the iron skillet with butter, when her hair spilled out of its ribbon and down her shoulders. She was back at home, probably up by now and filling the bird feeders with crumbling cakes of suet — sweet Gladys. She loved watching her woodpeckers, nuthatches, and juncos. He killed the motor and let the boat drift silently awhile. The quiet made him wish that Gladys was right there at his side with two cups of coffee and her playfully disapproving frown. He loved her so damn much. He closed his eyes and let the tranquility of the foggy marshland pulsate through him — so peaceful, so dreamy. It was another dip toward unconsciousness, but this time what snapped him awake was a sharp and unexpected cracking sound.

An immense branch had snapped not far from the bow, it's origin completely concealed by the billowing haze. This disturbance was followed by another loud snapping and what sounded like the low growl of a gray wolf. But this was certainly no damn wolf. The heavy tread alone indicated a much larger animal—probably a moose. Gary turned the ignition key. No response. He turned it again. There was a brief flutter of cogs, and then nothing at all. He had run out of fuel. At least the beastly disturbances stopped. He had never seen a moose out here, but it didn't mean it was impossible, just damn unusual. But that wasn't the only unusual thing. The mist-shrouded and unseen shore had fallen farther away from him on both sides. The channel unexpectedly widened. He could tell because the birds sounded farther away, and he could smell the peculiar blue aroma that larger rivers start to possess come April. It was as if the familiar channel had suddenly ruptured, and now there was an actual current that the boat eased along with. Gary had lost his bearings after all. He tried to jolt himself back to an awareness of his surroundings with a few vigorous head shakes. It was to no avail. He was lost.

But how could he be lost? These were his waters. At least they had been his waters. Now the landscape had inexplicably changed around him. This was an entirely different place. He heard a pattering of ducks taking flight in the distance. The familiar sound was heavy with the wetness of the fog, but unmistakably over a hundred yards behind him. He sensed the marshes regressing and receding. The current was noticeably stronger. He had somehow emerged on the slowly swirling eddies of an open bay, or maybe even the lake itself. The channel was gone. It had somehow dissolved away. Gary felt his eyelids grow heavy and quiver, and his hands slipped wetly from the wheel. He fell forward, and his chest turned the wheel hard to starboard. By the time he shuddered back up from his delirium, the old mahogany runabout had just completed a full circle and was heading starboard again. Gary reared back and corrected the course. Corrected? That didn't seem like the proper word for what he had done. He had just steered what he believed to be straight south into a swirling unknown.

If he ended up on Lake Beyond, it would be trouble later with the weather was expected to turn blustery and colder. There could even be some flurries thrown in by late afternoon. Gary had heard the weather report crackle forth from the transistor as he was getting ready in the mud room while Gladys snored back in bed. He was pulling on his boots, but the forecast gave him no real sense of urgency. There was plenty of time. Soon he was dressed and heading down to the boathouse. He knew he wasn't supposed to (Gladys would give him hell) but he had a cigarette along the way. The mist billowed around his smoking and concealed the transgression. It was a pack he had bought after getting out of the hospital. He had kept stowed it away until now. The tobacco tasted a little harsh and stale, and he only smoked half of it. When he unlocked the boathouse door and eased onto the runabout, he experienced such a wave of elation that tears gathered in his eyes. There had been bleak midwinter days when he thought he would never be home again. Now there he was. But that elation had all but evaporated because he no longer knew where he was. Dread crept in.

Then he heard the unexpected cawing and devious muttering of gathered crows. That must be an island, he thought. Might be a good idea to drop anchor close to shore and just wait for the fog to lift, he thought. It has to burn off with the sunrise. That was what he conjectured, but why did it seem to be getting thicker? And why did the sky seem to be getting darker? Had Gary set out pre-dawn and been drifting all day? Was that why he had run out of gas? Impossible. The fog should be long gone if that was the case, and the freezing rain would be falling. Just as he thought of this, a spray of icy pellets descended. Night was upon him, and the stubborn fog was finally breaking up. He could see the outline of that island of crows, and that was where he was drifting. Their cawing increased as he approached. Then an open shoreline came into view just past some tricky shoals, but Gary made it. He was awake and paying attention now. There would be protection in this little cove.

The logical decision, considering how damn tired he was, was to just pull in here and ride out the evening to another dawn. Or maybe search teams would come looking for him a lot sooner than dawn and they would find him all disoriented and shivering under his wool blankets—maybe an unlit cigarette dangling from his lips. Gary sure as hell didn't like the idea of sleeping on the runabout, but he knew the best thing to do when you get lost is find a safe place and stay put. Do something to draw attention to yourself when sufficient time has elapsed for the Coast Guard to set out. You will be found. How far could he have sailed? He could be in Canadian water past Chippewa Island, maybe even past the Great Spirit Islands. Either way there was no sense risking damage to the boat in unknown waters. Gary bundled himself up and remembered that he had brought some bourbon. A nip might be a good idea. And probably a smoke to pass the time. The nicotine and alcohol had the desired calming effect, and he found himself thinking of Gladys again. She must be worried sick. She also must be sore as hell. He took another molten swig and swished it around. He patted the steering wheel. He waited.

The Lost Canadian Birder

"So, this the only gas station in town?"

The elderly attendant behind the counter nodded. He was a stern-looking and severe cut of outdoorsman who remained eternally unimpressed when not in the wild. Getting answers out of him would be a challenge. Maybe.

"My name is Carl," the stranger continued. "Just pulled into town this morning. Never been through here before. Real peaceful."

The attendant repeated the same slow nodding of silent acknowledgment.

"What's your name?"

"Joe."

"Well, Joe. It's a pleasure to meet you. This is a beautiful area. Sad I haven't seen it until now. Must be some good fishing around here."

Joe the attendant crossed his arms impressively—confirming his status as the more strapping of the two—and sniffed. "You don't strike me as someone lookin' to fish."

"Maybe not," said Carl.

"We've got a pure stand of young jack pine that stretches over a hundred acres starting just up the road. Any chance that's where you're headed?"

Carl smiled. "I've heard they're back."

"Oh, they're back. They arrived two weeks ago."

"The Kirtland's warbler?"

Joe nodded. "Funny thing is—you don't seem like a birder, either."

Carl laughed. "You are very perceptive. I have city written all over me, don't I? You ever make it down to McKenzie?"

Joe shook his head slowly.

"Really nice place. I've been there almost ten years. Originally from Putorious, though."

The attendant soured further. "So, what are you looking for?"

"I'm looking for a man. Now he's a birder. He came up here looking for that warbler. About ten days ago."

"He ain't the only one. Lots of folks come through here looking for that bird. You got a picture?"

"I do," Carl kept smiling. "Right here on my phone. If you don't mind?"

Joe shrugged and thought, sure why not. When Carl held up his phone to scroll through the photos it didn't take many to flash by for the attendant to speak. "Sure, I saw that guy. That funny long hair. He filled his tank up here on his way through. Filled up my ears, too. French Canadian accent. He get lost or somethin'?"

Carl stopped smiling. "Or somethin'…"

"Said he was from Quebec. Real strong accent."

"That's Denis, the fella I'm looking for. He grew up in Canada, but he's been living down in McKenzie for about six years now. That's how I know him," Carl locked eyes with the attendant. "So how much did Denis tell you about where he was going?"

Joe spoke slowly. "Well, if you know him, then you must know how he talks."

"So much he can drive you crazy," Carl confirmed.

"You mind if I see your identification?"

Carl smiled. "I respect caution. Of course."

Joe inspected the driver's license Carl handed him and gave it back. "Sorry for asking, but I want to know for sure who I'm talking to. Just in case anything comes up later. I have a real good memory."

"So, you must remember what Denis said, or at least some of what he said. Any idea where he was headed?"

"Sure, I remember exactly what he told me. He was asking for directions to Maddy's house. She wrote a book about the Kirtland's warbler and lives just up the road."

Carl blinked a few times and then rubbed his eyes. "Sure sounds like somebody he'd want to talk to. So I guess that's where I should look then. Can you help me with directions?"

"Depends on how much you plan on bothering poor old Maddy."

Carl frowned. "Is she a frail woman?"

"She's older than me but she ain't frail. Just doesn't like to be bothered if it's not about birds."

"Well, this is kind of about the warbler. That's what Denis came to see."

"I suppose so. Just try not to upset her. If she

gets upset than we'll all pay for it long after you leave."

"Irritable old woman?" Carl asked.

"I wouldn't call her irritable, either. We just know that if she wants to talk, she'll come to us. Unless, like I said, it's a question specifically about birds. It's nice to have an expert around."

"She wrote a whole book about this bird?"

Joe said, "Yes, sir. I have a copy of it around here somewhere…"

"That's all right. She a retired professor or somethin'?"

The attendant took out an oily notepad from under the counter and began writing. "She worked over at Welldigger Bay College for years. Retired up here because she loved those little warblers so much. She even traveled down to the Bahamas in the winter a few times to see them. That's where they go. There's pine forests in the Bahamas. Never knew that until I met Professor Maddy." He tore off the sheet and handed it to Carl. "Here's where you'll find her. Don't tell her I told you, though. And don't bother her too much. She's got a brother who lives out there with her. It's about sixteen acres, mostly woodland. He stays in a cabin back in the woods. A little strange but he apparently helps her out. And he's pretty defensive about his older sister—real watchdog type."

Carl took the paper. "Thank you, sir. I promise to behave myself."

"So how do you know Denis?"

His smile flared back up "Oh, he's just a friend of mine."

"You a cop?" Joe asked.

"Do I look like a cop?"

"Maybe."

"Well, I'm not. And if you're wondering why the cops aren't looking for him, it's because they don't know he's missing. I think he would want me to find him first."

"He's in some kind of trouble."

Carl shrugged. "He would just get deported to Canada. He's done nothing criminal. He just neglected to do some necessary paperwork and now he is officially living here illegally. It's my intention to get it all straightened out for him once I can track him down."

"Maybe he was trying to disappear."

"That's a possibility. I will see what Maddy the ornithologist can tell me."

"Be nice."

"You have my word."

"And watch out for her brother," Joe warned.

Carl went back to grinning. "And let's hope he watches out for me."

The drive wasn't a terribly complicated one, but it did take him twenty minutes to get there. The last stretch was a poorly maintained gravel road winding through stands of vibrant, young jack pine—nearly all about twenty feet tall. Carl was passing through the site of a controlled burn conducted thirteen years ago. The trees were spaced out politely and this allowed for a fair amount of afternoon sun to fall on the spreading carpet of elegant and gently fluttering bracken fern below; fronds recently unfurled from their fiddleheads and freshly green triangular pinnate leaves glowing in the dappled shade. It was a scenic excursion for sure. But when making one final turn toward Maddy's house, he found a rusted pick-up truck parked lengthwise over the road. A man leaned against it with his arms crossed. This must be Maddy's brother, Carl thought.

Carl crunched and popped to a slowdown gravel stop then shifted to park. He kept the engine running and leaned out the window. "You must be Maddy's brother."

The man nodded slowly.

Carl brought his semi-automatic up with an effortless smooth motion. The following head shots sprayed the man's brains like vomit over the hood of his truck. Carl stepped out of his car and patted the silencer with gratitude. This was dry, sandy soil. And so quiet. Just the birds twittering their combinations of calls and songs. Carl wondered if any of these vocalizations belonged to the Kirtland's warbler. He dragged the body twenty feet into the concealing fern and pulled the truck off the road. When he was done, he kicked some gravel and dust over the most obvious bits of gore. There was a raven, nearly two feet long from bill to tail, watching him from a jack pine perch above. The bird cocked its head in various inquisitive angles and then took flight with a croaking complaint when an annoyed Carl drew his gun again. He put it away without firing another shot and continued his drive. It wasn't long before he came upon the house of the ornithologist. It wasn't much, just a five-room cabin. The front door was open. All the windows were open too. He heard the sound of a woman softly singing when he got out of his car—and then a shout.

"You must be the one looking for Denis."

Carl studied the windows but saw no one. "Yes, ma'am."

"Joe phoned me."

"I told him not to."

"Well, you're here now so come on in."

When Carl entered, he found her sitting in the humid dark of the front room. She was reclined in a rocker with an old bulky tape player on her lap. On the low table in front of her was a green teapot flanked by two matching cups resting on what appeared to be an antique platter. "Do you take tea?"

Carl smiled his widest smile. "That would be wonderful."

"Then we could talk between sips."

He nodded. "Of course. May I sit down?"

"By all means. So, my name is Madeleine," she told him as she poured. "And you caught me at a good time. I can talk for one cup of tea but then I'm afraid you must go. There is a lot I have to do around here before the sun sets."

"But you have a good four hours of sunlight left."

She licked thin, wrinkled lips. "It will be here before you know it."

"I thought you had your brother out here to help you?"

Maddy frowned. "He's a lot less help than he used to be."

"Understood. Well, my hope is that this won't take long at all."

Maddy seemed to have lost interest in their exchange after mention of her brother. She suddenly looked tired. She slumped and mumbled. "I haven't seen your Denis in more than a week. My assumption was that he just moved on. He was staying at the Red Cedar Motel on the other side of town."

"He stayed there two nights. Never checked out."

Maddy handed him his teacup. "Then he must have moved on. He isn't camping on my land if that's what you've been led to believe."

"Not at all. I have the same assumption—that he just moved on. I'm just wondering if he mentioned where he might be headed. Did he find the bird he was looking for?"

"At least one of them—the Kirtland's warbler."

"Did he mention any others? I know he had a checklist."

"He indeed had a checklist. I suggested a few modifications, in fact. So yes, I do know what bird he set out to find when he left. It was my suggestion, after all."

"Yeah?"

She nodded. "Why, yes."

"So, what was it?"

Maddy the ornithologist demurred with an exaggerated dainty hand. "Please, sir. Try your tea."

Carl took a smell and a sip. "Delicious. Flowery."

"I must say I'm a bit surprised that you like tea

at all."

Carl thought about his gun. It still seemed warm from the last time it fired. In fact, it seemed to be inexplicably getting warmer. A bead of sweat formed on his brow. He took another sip of the tea to calm himself. "Damn delicious."

"It's my own brew. Named after the bird your friend went looking for—the yellow-crested bogflutter."

Carl squinted. "Never heard of that one."

"They are a more secret resident of these woods. How familiar are you with birds?"

"I would say I know the basics."

"Do you know your finches?"

"I know what a goldfinch looks like."

She smiled. "Spirited little birds with that lovely looping flight. Everyone knows them. But our yellow-crested bogflutter is much more similar in behavior to the purple finch. I just had the pleasure of keeping a flock of purple finches on my property over the winter. Do you know what a flock of finches is called?"

"I can't say that I do…"

"A charm. Isn't that appropriate? Well, I had a charm of finches right here. That flat table-style feeder you may have noticed on your way up the walk was full of their fluttering until the first snow-melting rains arrived in March. The departure of the finches coincided with the arrival of a nesting pair of bogflutters."

"Really?" He sipped his tea more deeply. The gun burning so close to his skin seemed to urge him on.

"I see you're taken with my bogflutter tea."

"It's quite good. So where do you think Denis went?"

"I told you. He went looking for the bird. They have a much more limited range once they find a conifer branch suitable for their tightly-woven cup nest. And once they have a clutch of eggs to protect, they don't wander far and they certainly never visit feeders. So, he had to go deeper into the woods to find them. I had a general idea where they were nesting and he seemed confident in his abilities to get there and back."

"Do you think you could tell me how to get

there?"

"If you're not used to navigating by compass it could get tricky. It's a five-mile hike from my doorstep, no trail. And it's certainly nothing you want to begin this late in the day. I suppose he could be camping out there. I honestly have not been back there since I gave him those instructions."

Carl pondered this, sipping and pondering and sipping. Damn delicious tea. "You suppose you could lead me out there in the morning?"

"You are already on your way."

"What?"

"You are already on your way if you're looking for the yellow-crested bogflutter."

Carl let the teacup fall. A wave of faintness misted his vision and blurry hands reached for a gun but couldn't find it before he dropped to his knees. Not that he would have had the focus to fire it effectively anyway. He was going down. In fact, soon he was flat on the floor. Maddy kept talking— standing up and walking over to leer above him slantwise and foggy with that old bulky tape player in her hands.

"Let me tell you more about this bird you will be seeing," she was saying. "Let me tell you a bit more about the yellow-crested bogflutter. Let me play you a tape I made of their trickling song."

Maddy pushed play. The recording began and instantly drew Carl, with more backwards gravity, to greater depths. All was dark at first. There was only that sound, a solitary bird at first, warming as if in pre-dawn with a soft purring twitter that grew bolder by degree as some unseen sun was on the rise. The further he descended, the louder it became. It was soon joined by the vocalizations of several birds. In a fleeting moment of clarity, the murderous Carl realized that these were not recordings of actual birds at all, but instead recordings of Maddy the ornithologist mimicking birds. Above him, she chirped along with the tape that played. One last breach into consciousness found her still there—her leer intensifying into true predatory malice.

You damn fool, he thought, you have supped tainted tea with some kind of foul woodland spellcaster, and this, sir, means you are in deep shit. The revelation dissolved, and soon he was back to just listening, back to his slow-motion descent. This is the song of the yellow-crested bogflutter, he realized. The first spirited metallic chirps he heard repeated variations of the same twinkling phrase. Carl wondered if a group of bogflutters would be called a charm as well, and he fell—drifting further and further down in a whirlpool of wings that came close enough to brush his forehead and cheeks. The chirps passed right by his ears. There was a feeble trace of orange sunrise visible somewhere. The flying of the birds, still moving much too fast to see in any detail, seemed to line a dimly lit tunnel that went downwards. It was as if he were dropping into a funnel cloud of beating wings. This was an oblivion float, a weightlessness, a forgetfulness. The stranger was crowded by birdsong—ever growing in intensity—until eventually there seemed to be the clamor of hundreds of bogflutters all singing at once. A lavish, oscillating chorus whipped warmly around him and tugged him down—a rara avis chavish, an unexpected aviary—until he felt no falling or flesh at all.

The Cabin on Bogflutter Lake

The tranquility was typical of a midsummer sundown on Bogflutter Lake—the aloft buzzing of the cicadas replaced by the new fervent insect chatter of evening, the still dripping canoe pulled across the taller grasses on the shore and shining sunburst orange in the fading afternoon, oars at rest in the sandy dirt, the haunted high-sailing night song of the loons commencing, a newly constructed fire crackling in the old fire pit, the wood wet and smoking, and then the sighing of a cool breeze in the pine. Billy sat alone on the edge of the little dock with a freshly lit joint between his fingers—taking it all in.

Sure, it was a tragedy that those people were murdered across the lake, but all indications pointed to the incomprehensible randomness of a serial killer passing through. Nothing had happened since. Nothing would. That was three goddamn years ago. Billy sure didn't like to think about what that family must've experienced in their final hours, shot with

84

arrows, dismembered, and left scattered about in the leaf litter and fallen pine needles. He remembered that one of the hands, belonging to the husband, had been found not twenty feet from the dock on which he sat—transported and nibbled on by some indiscriminate critters. Those damn murders wouldn't ruin Bogflutter Lake for Billy. This was his. The families who owned the other three cabins had never returned after the bloodshed, and now they sat empty. This place, the old family cabin, was his. Bogflutter Lake was his. The ghostly wailing of the loons belonged to him.

All this serenity was his to enjoy, and this was where he would be all the damn time if he didn't have to work—fishing and paddling around, drinking beer, and smoking reefer on this familiar perch when the day finally wound down. He would listen to old country music, and keep the rifle and the shotgun clean. He would watch the ducks flap across the water, and watch the summer turn solemnly to rusted and rainy fall. Then came the deep white winters of chopping wood, snowmobiles, and ice fishing. He took a drag and closed his eyes. Thoughts of cleaning fish with his father were carrying him adrift when he heard someone step clumsily onto the dock behind him.

He turned. It was Darla. "Be careful, honey."

"This is so goddamn rickety and dangerous. Did your father put together this claptrap shit?" Billy asked.

"I know he tried to fix it a few times. Grandpa built it."

Darla sat down next to him. She was wearing her neatly tied, red head scarf to collect her savagely dyed red hair. Her features were relaxed and ruddy from canoe explorations and lake water swimming beyond the duckweed. "Enjoying a quiet moment?"

"Clearing my head. How's your leg?"

Darla displayed her tattooed shin to him. "Just a couple leeches. It'll be all right."

Billy nodded and thought about taking another hit, but realized he was high enough and did not wish to ascend beyond the ability to converse. He stalled, just looking at the dwindling joint, beholden to its potency.

"Can I have a hit of that?"

He grinned and passed it over. "No need to ask, sweetheart. You finish it off. But don't let Freddy see you."

"Shit, that guy is a real asshole, right?"

"I told you we should have come alone."

"Eve is my best friend," said Darla.

"That is absolutely true. But Eve tends to date fucking dipshits. What's he doing in there anyway?" Billy asked.

"I believe the uncultured brute is drinking some of your whiskey and saying that he has had enough of this sitting around the lake garbage and that he's headed into town to that little bar, whatever the fuck it's called."

"Heading into town? He's such a tease."

"No, I really think he's going."

"Barney going with him?" Billy asked.

"Freddy said he wants to go alone," replied Darla.

"Did he say it like Greta Garbo?"

"Exactly like Greta Garbo."

Darla smiled, and when Darla smiled everything was better. On the other side of the cabin they heard

Freddy's 1959 Buick LeSabre roar into gravel, spraying life. The sound was followed by the distinctive angry puttering of the dual exhaust. It was a beautiful car. That was what had foolishly convinced Billy to let the asshole drive. That big trunk and torpedo brake lights and factory dash and fins. Now it was roaring off down Bogflutter Road to town; leaving them stranded.

"Guess he really wanted to get out of here," Billy remarked.

"He doesn't like you, Billy."

Billy took the joint back from her. It had gone out, so he tucked it in his shirt pocket for safekeeping. "I know he doesn't like me because I smoke jazz cigarettes."

Darla scooted next to him and put her head on his shoulder. "I'm sorry, Billy. We'll still have a good time. And we can always come back some other weekend, maybe at the end of August?"

"We should've come alone."

She nodded. "It would certainly be easier to fuck."

"Oh, yeah?"

"Oh, yeah."

Darla placed a chipped fingernail suggestively to her pout. "I think that's something we should take care of right now."

"Where?"

"One of the empty cabins. Maybe the murder cabin?"

He shook his head. "It's too far and there's not much left anyway. Locals burned most of it down. How about the old Johnson place? At least it still has a roof."

She bit her lip. "But the murder cabin would be exciting."

"We're not walking that far tonight. The Johnson place is really the furthest I'm willing to go. Besides, there are storms rolling in. Feel that sweet phantasmal breeze?"

She tapped him on the nose. "I will get you to fuck me out by the murder cabin."

Billy shrugged. "I suppose you will. But tonight, it's the Johnson place..."

Freddy should not have been driving. But

Freddy did a lot of things he wasn't supposed to do. He was the type of belligerent gearhead greaser prone to miscalculation. Not only did he drive, but he drove angrily, bouncing on the rough forest road, headlights flashing in the trees. All of a sudden, the front whitewall on the passenger's side blew in a rapid spluttering, and he spun to a stop with a flurry of curses. Goddamn fuck, that's a two-hundred-dollar tire, and all I wanted was a beer on a barstool. He killed the engine and whipped the keys out of the ignition. As soon as Freddy stepped out onto the road, the mosquitoes were on him. He cursed some more. This was a swampy section of woods. He stormed around to assess the damage, and was stunned by the sight of an arrow lodged in the shredded treads of his tire. It had struck the front. Someone had let it fly from almost head on. From the front. Head on.

By the time Freddy figured that whoever shot the arrow had probably done so right from the particular section of swampy woods where he now stood, there was a hiss in the air and a thudding in his back. The strike grazed the right side of his heart and cracked a rib. He fell. And when he twisted painfully to look behind him, he saw a smiling man in military green—hairless and pale as a maggot—coming towards him with a rope looped over one arm. From the other arm swayed an open noose. The lurching and hunched aggression of the attacker, combined with his strength, made Freddy feel as though he were being manhandled by a bear in his final moments. Sometimes, men get killed by black bears in these woods, the most docile of all North American bears. Sometimes men get killed by them. These were his thoughts as the noose dropped over his head. When he was shoved down, he deflated, as if the arrow still lodged in his breast had punctured him like a balloon. Freddy's face was pushed into the dirt while his attacker used the other end of the noose to tie his hands behind his back in a slipknot that cut into the skin of his wrists. This was followed by a brutal teeth-chipping rag in his mouth which prevented him from screaming once the archer turned to butcher and the sawing began behind his left kneecap.

When Billy and Darla were finished trading orgasms in the old Johnson place, they wandered dreamily back. Eve and Barney were sitting suspiciously close together on the old army cot by the fire. It was clear to both couples that the others had just enjoyed the same level of lakeside intimacy. Night had fallen. In the distance came the fusillade booming of nocturnal thunder. The dark sky flashed.

"No Freddy?"

Eve shook her head. "Nope."

"You better hope he doesn't come back and find the two of you so cozy."

Barney was not much smarter than his gearhead friend. He stared with boozy indifference into the flames while Eve tugged on his arm. "We were just having a little fun."

"Freddy is a goddamn hothead," said Barney.

"Oh, fuck him," Eve snarled. "He's been a real jerk since we got up here…"

Billy agreed but still did not approve. "I really came up here to relax. You are not making it easy."

"Don't worry about it."

Billy shrugged. "I hope there's some beer left."

Barney awkwardly spoke up. "Sure, man, there's plenty."

The old greaser squinted. "What do you think your friend would do if he found you with his woman?"

Barney laughed through his nose. "Guess he'd have to deal with it."

Darla intervened. "Billy, go get yourself a beer. Bring me one, too."

When Billy went into the cabin Darla glared. "This is his goddamn family cabin. The two of you should show more respect. I hope you had the decency to not fuck inside."

"On the table," Eve grinned.

In the closer woods there was the sound of branches snapping—something moving without caution in the lower tangles of the brush. The three of them listened. Thunder boomed again. Then came a loud crack of lightning, followed by the hiss of night rain in the pines. They abandoned the fire and hurried inside.

"So, you think Freddy made it back into town

before the storm hit?"

"You've seen the way he drives."

Billy ran a hand through the collapsing, greasy mess of his hair. "We should have taken two cars. I mean, I should have taken my truck. What if he decides to be a dick and stay in town?"

Eve stood up and rifled through her purse for a pack of cigarettes. "I thought it was nice of him to volunteer to drive, but if he decides to be a dick and strand us here, there will be hell to pay. Hell. To. Pay."

This threat brought Billy no comfort. "I have to say one thing about you, Eve. You are consistent."

"What is that supposed to mean?"

"It means you are always seeking the same dynamic."

She sneered. "I'm heading out for a smoke. Anyone care to join me?"

When there were no takers, she flipped them all off and went onto the porch alone. It was enclosed with a screen where countless, crusted remnants of dead insects had gathered in the stapled corners. It offered just enough protection from the sprays of gusty rain to keep her mostly dry. The downpour was raging and loud. Just as she maneuvered her cupped lighter to the tip of her smoke, there was a breathtaking flash of lightning coupled with the crackling of split timber. The flash revealed a world of furious torrents, swaying conifer boughs. and a skull in the trees—was that a human skull in the trees? Then the electricity went out. There was no generator.

Eve heard the others groan inside.

Strange thing to see what appeared to be a skull.

In those blowing trees . . .

It seemed so unreal. She disregarded it. Eve had five different skulls tattooed on her body, after all. It was only natural that she would see them every so often. She turned her back to the rain and cupped her hand around the lighter once more. If the power was out, it would be back on soon enough. Why waste the time worrying about it? She lit up, puffed, and bounced up and down on her toes. She swiveled her hips back and forth. She still felt horny. That was always what got her into trouble. She didn't like to wait when she was in these moods, and stupid

Freddy had been making her wait. It was why she had three divorces in her wake and why she would never exchange vows again. She took a deeper drag and thought of Freddy. He wasn't a keeper. He wasn't even much of a fuck—his simpleton garage buddy had just bested him in that department. The distracted Eve swiveled her hips some more when she thought of how surprisingly large Barney was. An endowed simpleton at least. There was another bright flash of lightning, but this time she saw no skull. She just kept smoking until ashes met filter, and then went back inside.

The morning broke all misty and aglow with bird chatter. Billy was snoring. Darla could hear that the rain had stopped, so she slid out of bed naked, wrapped herself in a beach towel, grabbed a bar of soap and her little travel bottle of shampoo, then headed down to the lake. While making her exit, she tested a light switch. Power was still out. She also looked out the front window to see if Freddy had ever returned, but there was no Buick. She assumed he would be slithering his way back sometime in the early afternoon with a hangover and possibly a new venereal disease. Darla actually breathed a sigh of relief. Having a respite from him was nice. And Billy was right—next time, they would just come up here alone. Next time they would even take the following Monday off, and maybe even call in sick on Tuesday. Next time would be more romantic. She smiled. Everything outside was still dripping, and from the far distance came the soft roar of distant thunder.

The storm had rattled the woods for a solid six hours before moving on. It had poured so much, in fact, that flooding was likely, and maybe that was the reason Freddy hadn't returned. Maybe Bogflutter Road is covered with overflowing swamp water. Maybe his tires are wedged in mud and his wait for the tow truck is taking longer than expected. Maybe he's there leaning against the hood, chain-smoking and snarling. Darla willed herself to think no more of irritable Freddy. Instead, she focused on her barefoot tiptoe over freshly fallen branches and puddles. Once on the dock, she finally took a breath to admire Bogflutter Lake. The black, placid surface of the water hardly moved beneath the hovering, and now dispersing, mist. There was no lapping at the shore. The only ripples came from sunrise bluegill occasionally snatching something from the surface. One bigger splash further in the lake could have been a largemouth bass, or even a diving loon. But that was it. All was otherwise still.

Darla stepped carefully down the slippery length of the dock. She was humming lightly when she dropped her towel, set down her accessories, and carefully descended into the chill of the water. After catching her breath, she lunged forward and swam a few strokes out. The water carried the shivers of recent rainfall and moon-glow. She popped back up and smeared the wetness and hair from her eyes. She stretched a toe down and felt the vegetated bottom. She felt something large swimming near her, and she remembered Billy telling her that he had seen a bowfin at least a foot long in the shallows the previous morning. He said that at first he thought it was an eel down there in the murk, but then it spun and he saw the distinctive bony-plated head. Darla loved the sound of the words associated with Billy's cabin. She liked saying bowfin and bluegill, cinnamon fern and tufted loosestrife, hemlock and black ash, tamarack and groundwater seepage, and roof moss and hibachi. She liked the idea of living here with Billy full-time someday. Too bad they could never have kids. Kids would love this place. She splashed water on herself and let her mind drift to the moments they would have. Billy strapping a tiny life preserver on his daughter. Their daughter's own little fishing pole. Billy smiling as he lifted her into the canoe for the first time. Then later showing her how to fold pumpkinseed fillets into tinfoil for the first time. How to build and tend a fire for the first time. And those murders that happened across the lake would be their summertime campfire story, and each year it would get more outlandish and gruesome. A daughter to bring a husband here, and maybe even children of her own. Darla wiped a saltier wetness from her eyes and made her way slowly back to the dock for soap and shampoo. She saw Billy coming out of the cabin, searching for her. They waved to one another and Billy made his way over, swatting mosquitoes.

"No Freddy?"

"No."

"No car?"

"No, sir."

Billy was grinning widely. "And still no electricity?"

"I don't think so."

"And no bra or panties?"

Darla shook her head. "Absolutely not."

"I could sure use some black coffee."

"Campfire coffee is your only option."

"Damn fire pit is soaked." Billy thought of something and nodded. "Good morning for a hike around the lake. Maybe by the time we get back we'll have power."

"Sounds cool to me. Maybe all the way to the murder cabin?"

Billy conceded. "Sure. But taking Bogflutter Road is not an option. That would add over two miles going there and back. We'll have to take the trail. And we'll have to bring our mud boots."

Darla wrote a note for the still-slumbering Eve and Barney while Billy shoved some supplies, including a modest lunch for both of them, into his old green backpack. This was followed by big hissing clouds of repellent in the screened porch, while the birds chattered and a pair of wood ducks splashed in flight away from something. Billy thought he heard a mechanical sound, maybe even the approaching hum of Freddy's car, but after a closer listen he could pinpoint nothing unusual—just the morning chorus of the midsummer lake.

"You sure you want to hike all the way to the murder cabin?" Billy asked.

"Sure I'm sure," said Darla.

"It's three miles there and three miles back."

"I've been down most of that trail before."

"Not since what happened. I don't know if you remember that last stretch, but it transitions from a dry forest to a pine and hardwood swamp pretty quickly. Should be extra swampy after all that rain."

Darla pointed to her bulky hiking boots. "I think these will work."

So, the two of them trudged off down the trail. The clouds lingered and the mosquitoes were bad, but every so often there was a break in the canopy and a break in the overcast. In those spaces, they could feel the humidity start to build. Both were sweating before they made the first mile, but at least that part of the trail followed a slight ridge over a sandy glacial outwash plain and was surprisingly dry. Billy took a lot of pride in pointing out the trees, so she humored him with politely manufactured curiosity. He drew her attention to the black spruce and the balsam fir. There were a few white pines. Lots of paper birch. And here, he told her, here is a northern red oak that must be eighty feet tall. Seeing that particular tree had always signaled a break. The spreading branches, so far aloft, had managed to clear quite an area below, and the old coarsely grained trunk was a fine place to lean a backpack. That's what Billy did. Then he sat down.

"I love this tree."

"How old do you think it is?"

"It's easily a hundred years old. I can remember, for a couple summers in my youth, there was a tire swing hanging off one of the branches. Not even the rope is left. The Johnson kids might've put it up."

"You had a lot of fun up here?"

He nodded. "Sure enough."

"So, you never knew the people who got killed?"

"Saw the father on the lake fishing twice that I can recall. Just waved. Never spoke to him. Men don't go fishing to talk."

"Neither do women."

He was still looking up when he heard something moving in the leaves of the unseen brush. There were lots of shrubs around them—serviceberry, bunchberry, witch-hazel, and what looked like huckleberry. The bushy branches of the huckleberry quivered. Billy put a finger to his lips and pointed. They both watched for quite some time, but the branches never moved again, and no creature emerged. They decided to get back on the trail. Billy and Darla didn't talk much. They just listened and retreated into their thoughts. For Billy, his thoughts were increasingly drawn to the murder cabin, especially once the trudge of their boots had carried them into the mires and mud that signaled they were drawing near.

This was the place where four lives had been extinguished—one of them a child of seven. This was the place where four torsos, decorated by arrows as if they were pin cushions, had been chained to adjacent red pines—the bark below darkened by gore, the fluttering wings of inquisitive birds, the snooping and sniffing of black bears—eventually old man Johnson fishing in the weeds offshore, reeling in and releasing a handsome pike before taking note of the atrocities on display around the cabin. And then the flashing of lights, body bags, and yellow tape. One car after another raised the gravel dust from the bumps and turns of Bogflutter Road. Billy himself returned to the lake just two weeks after the killings. What had been a peaceful retreat since childhood had been fucking debauched. The thick trunk of every older tree loomed ominous with the possibility of a concealed psychopath. Of course, the killer had not been caught. The killer had never been caught. And the trail had grown cold. But similar lakeside murders in Wisconsin and then Minnesota suggested the evil had followed a natural progression and moved west. Billy recalled how he shuddered when first opening the cabin door, and how a chill from this shuddering lingered through the following methodical investigation of the rooms. Thankfully the butcher who had created such a nauseating display on the other side of the water had left Billy's cabin unscathed. Billy calmed down once he knew each room and closet was clear and once he was brewing coffee with his shotgun on the kitchen table next to a jar of freshly opened Hoppe's. Billy remembered.

"Is that it?" Darla called.

He looked up. It was.

"Spooky."

He nodded in agreement. It sure was. The roof had collapsed after the arson attempts and nearly the entire porch had been dismantled. Grasses and saplings sprouted everywhere in the wreckage. It was as if the locals had exhausted themselves enough while punishing the house to be satisfied and then staggered off. What they left behind was little more than an eyesore frame with blackened walls. The structure would never sufficiently shelter another human being again. With an unnecessarily polite slowness, the teeming gravity of the landscape was pulling it to the ground. Soon it would be unrecognizable. Soon the forest would engulf it.

"Not much of it left, eh?" Darla said.

"Not enough to make your dream come true."

Darla wiped the back of her neck and then used the same rag to swat at a deer fly. "Well, not unless you want to prop me up on that fallen crossbeam."

"Doesn't seem safe to me."

"Not at all."

Then they both heard it. The distinctive angry puttering of dual exhaust. Freddy's big old cruiser was coming back down Bogflutter Road.

The Sandy River Man

He awoke, shirtless and hung over in an unfamiliar hayloft, far from the river. Seemed he had made an effort to get as far from flowing water as possible. He smelled the faded whiskey on the tatters of his shirt and his jeans were stiff with a shellac of dried mud. They cracked when he moved, causing little slow-motion flakes to drift like dust away from him. Not just any dust, but stardust. The Sandy River Man gazed at these drifting flakes in wonder, seemingly unable to fully shed the peculiar fabrications of sleep. It felt as though he was still in slumber. But the boards beneath him were unyielding, and the foul breath he exuded was pungent. This was at least partial wakefulness. Maybe it was as awake as he could get. Maybe he had been drugged. Maybe it was just the fucking humidity. It made it so hard for a man to gather his thoughts. What he knew for certain was that he had been rained on last night and, somewhere in his pursuit of shelter, had blacked out.

And now the sun was rising through the cracked and red-chipped paint of hayloft doors. The Sandy River Man was far from his river. Far from where he had left his canoe.

He propped himself up on one elbow and regarded a sunrise all gloriously swollen and blood orange: late August. It bore a punishing weight. Of course, he had enjoyed his long summer — casting lines, pitching tents, and paddling along from one sexual river conquest to the next. The river kept him fed, after all. But the river also kept him hungry, and it had been a long season of exhausting appetites. It was too goddamn hot and too goddamn humid. He was ready for the first hard frost — the one that extinguishes the ragweed and goldenrod for good, the one that hardens the landscape and produces the first substantial leaf drop. He longed for the quiet celibacy of snowfall that would follow; his beloved river would be fringed with ice and all the ponds would be frozen. But it seemed so far away, and there certainly was more fucking to be done.

The day the Sandy River Man awoke shirtless and hung over in an unfamiliar hayloft was shaping up to be the most humid day of the season. The inferno heat was intensifying. He felt it. Behind his eyes there was a throbbing that made it hard to look in the light, so he didn't. Instead he shut his eyes tight. He strained to remember just what the hell had happened the night before. The air was fogged and growing thicker. Must already be over eighty degrees. There had been those storms last night. That was the one thing he could remember, were those tree-cracking storms, the electric flashing, and the running and the slipping into big puddles. Where had he been running from? The river. Who had he been running from?

As memories were hazily restored, he felt the growing presence of a woman. He had been on yet another debauch somewhere back toward Hillcreek. He had come across a woman wading, dress lifted to just below her knees revealing unnaturally pale cerulean calves. It was as if she had just crawled from some saturated beaver lodge of aspen and willow. The sight of her made every muscle in his body flex with tension, but when he tried to focus on her features, the memory was misted over so completely he could barely recall her at all. There had been flashes of lightning. He had pulled the canoe ashore — not for portage, but for shelter. Another flash of lightning and the woman walked toward him, dripping an oily trail in the water. The embankment had been steeper than expected. His boots had been slipping, and for some reason he had failed to mark the approaching storms as the threat they clearly were. And there had been the dewy distraction of her. And he was pretty sure she had fucked him more completely than whiskey ever could.

The Sandy River Man, instinctively concerned with the integrity of his manhood after such bender depravation, reached a hand down to his crotch and inspected. It was an old anxiety of his that had followed him through most of his drunken life — the fear that one morning he would wake up after blacking out and discover his cock and balls vandalized in some fashion or, heaven forbid, removed entirely. He needed his package intact. One day, he was going to clean up and maybe meet the right woman and have a family. He had to keep himself in general working condition until then. Thankfully, his inspection revealed nothing awry. In fact, the Sandy River Man was engorged to full salute.

He felt around in the hay surrounding him and found the neck of a bottle full of whatever he had been drinking the previous evening. When he tilted it forward, a shimmering cascade of blue stars fell out. They sizzled briefly upon landing, then vanished. They were remnants of an enchanted summer evening beyond recollection, where he had buried his cock in at least one dripping sanctuary along the river. This was nothing new for him, of course. His canoe wanderings were legendary, and any woman camping alone near the riverbank during his gliding excursions would likely have to fend off his advances. There were husbands and boyfriends from Hillcreek to Muscoda who wanted to fill the Sandy River Man with buckshot. But the woman he had been with the previous evening was no one's bride. He was sure of it. He was also sure she had drugged him. His confusion was surely the result of more than just the goddamn humidity. She had been on top. He remembered now. Flashes of their sopping union blazed before him, and he remembered she had been on top and was a magnificent rider. Great splashes of water as she hammered him on the riverbank. The bloody river stone marks on his sore ass stood as testimony to the fury he had been subjected to. What the hell kind of whiskey had he been drinking? The Sandy River Man looked back at the blue star bottle to check the label. It melted over his hand like candle wax, so he flung it away. The slurping thud it made on the hayloft rafters inspired a scattering of crows outside. He scowled from the strain of failed remembrance and rose angrily to his feet. This disorientation was undignified. It was going to be a long, hot day and he had to get back to his canoe. It was time to get moving.

Once outside, the misted radiance of the sun came glaring hot, orange through the humid air. The Sandy River Man surveyed his surroundings. He noted the ruins of a farmhouse across the field. It was missing its roof, and the remaining walls were charred black and crawling in fluttering creepers—it was abandoned. That was why he had chosen the barn, no doubt. Or maybe he had just gotten lucky. Maybe he had been taken here by that woman. What woman? No matter. He tried to focus on his immediate challenge. He was filthy and thirsty and had to find water. He walked past the wreckage of the place—past rusted farm machinery and desiccated livestock carcasses glittering with busy flies. He could feel the moisture beading on his forehead as he staggered along. And when he crossed the gravel country road and looked slantwise in both directions, he saw no other homestead in sight. But there was a shallow stream in the distance, and he followed the stream back to his river.

The banks of the Sandy were steep, and the water was flowing strong from the storms. The insects were crackling loudly around him. He waded in and washed himself a bit and then—just after taking handfuls of water into his mouth and finding it pungent—he looked upstream and saw a spidery giant of a man pissing into the current that swirled to where he crouched. The monstrous beast must have stood eleven feet tall and looked very much like an insect itself—even the way its head swiveled so freely, eyes shimmering black with innumerable compound facets. The legs hinged back and forth on their spindly joints, and with a hiss of annoyance the creature removed his lower mandible and tomahawked it toward the Sandy River Man, who watched helpless as it swept through the air in slow motion to vanish with a wisp of incineration into his abdomen. Then he felt his midsection collapse in a hissing whisper of hot ashes. The whisper of hot ashes ascended until it broke above him in the same blue stars that rushed from his bottle. They sizzled and burned up in the heat.

It was time to move on, so he continued walking, following the riverbank. The sun punished him, and perspiration poured from his brow. When he wasn't looking, his foot caught a fallen branch, and down he sailed into spluttering unconsciousness. Once consumed in this new oblivion, he began to make out shapes—the flapping retreat of a brook trout over interstellar riffles flared up, then the massive flapping of a sandhill crane, and the flapping of lady fern tapestries, the flapping of an outboard motor, the flapping of movement down the river. When he snapped awake, the humidity was so strong that he noticed he was now waterlogged, shirt plastered against his sore back. He was breathing heavy. A strange and unexpected night had fallen. The Sandy River Man was now standing on a majestically open bend of the river he knew well, and she was swelling her banks. Her rippling surface was mesmerizing—a black, glassy flatness of lightly rippling waves lit by a full moon that was slowly alternating in color from purplish deep-blue to lavender to red and back again. The water below pulsated with this preternatural light. The Sandy River Man looked down, and the ground was swimming around his boots. At first, he thought he had stepped onto a migration of snakes, but then the interlocking weave of movements beneath him were revealed to be nothing more than floodwater. Floodwater!

The revelation caused a rise of panic, but then he saw her—a silhouette seated on the shore straight ahead. The seductress who had lured him here the night before. He had tried to run away. He had made it all the way to that unfamiliar hayloft. But she had serenaded him back for another night. And on how many nights before that? The humidity swelled around him and his eyelids fluttered. He looked at her — long, sandy-blonde hair spilled over naked shoulders — and a force emanated from her that suggested the entire nocturnal landscape, everything from the humidity to the moon above was responsive to her charms. She smiled at him and opened her legs.

Great Hemlock Island

The strange, high whistling seemed to be coming from everywhere now. He paused his paddling for a moment and rested the dripping oars on his knees, drifting ahead to the deeper lake waters on a tide that flowed strong and in his favor. Such strange, high whistling. The sound of nocturnal rising. The sound of massive, intangible shapes as they misted from the forest floors, cedar swamps, and placid bays. The whistling jostled the green needle heights of balsam fir and tamarack, and sent roosting night birds into spastic evasive flight. The canoe drifted. He whistled in his own way to encourage the night chorus he sailed through. It moved in rippling tremors under his skin. Eventually, these forces gained enough invisible substance to press the trees sideways, exposing a muscular gargantuan bulk. He rubbed his bearded chin. Dark red flakes from the dried blood that covered his face fell away. He had smeared himself from the fountain that bubbled from his victim's chest and — once he had smeared himself — felt like a warrior. When he stood up afterwards in his new crimson mask, he noticed that the whistling he had heard on the night of his arrival had grown stronger or, rather, his consciousness had been sufficiently expanded by his bloody deed in order to perceive it more clearly. He had opened himself up.

His flesh was burning from the great effort his spirit was making to escape, and although his previous life had assumed a misted and remote quality, he found himself vaguely remembering past whistlings. He remembered once seeing an old sailor standing on the edge of a dock looking over a tranquil harbor to the sea, whistling an ominous and lonesome-sounding invitation to the winds that never seemed to arrive. He remembered a tattooed wayfarer being reprimanded by punches and kicks for whistling lewdly at the wrong woman in a Red Jacket bar, and also the way his cousin had musically chirped his way from one room to another whenever visiting, as if every movement demanded melodic accompaniment. He himself once whistled a lot of old country tunes and television jingles, but none of these whistlings compared to what this blood-soaked dugout rider was hearing now. His hunting knife was lying at his feet. It had not been cleaned. Both hands of his victim, severed at the wrist, were lying at his feet as well, bound together like captured tarantulas in a thick wrapping of twine. It was an offering. It must be delivered. He lifted his oars by the badly worn grips and paddled on.

"Did you hear that?"

"What?"

"That's the great barred owl."

"I know . . ."

"I love that call. Sounds like he's asking . . ."

"Who cooks for you?"

"Yeah."

"Seems like you always hear them more in the spring, though."

"Mating season."

"Right. It's their mating season."

She studied her bearded companion for a long moment and took one final pull on their bogflutter joint. It was spent. She tucked the roach away carefully while he poked a twig into the fire and marveled at the throbbing embers that crackled to cast up a rising corkscrew column of quickly diminishing orange sparks. He followed them with his eyes until they lost their glow and fell apart into curling ash in the air they vacated. Directly over the hundred-foot pine that crowned the enclosure of their campsite, he saw the hollowed-out crescent of a late summer moon. The owl hooted his question again, and was answered from across the lake by the strange undulating wail of a single loon, still sleek and wet from his cold-water night diving.

"This island really does seem haunted."

He blinked and sniffled. He poked at the fire again. "I don't know."

"I think it is. I know it is."

He shrugged, and then suddenly remembered he had an open bottle of beer twisted into the sandy ground next to him. He picked it up and took a long drink while something large moved through the trees behind them, paused briefly, then continued on its way. The low breeze carried a musky smell.

"It's a deer," he whispered.

"I know," she mockingly whispered back to him. "You're funny."

"Why?"

"You really don't want to talk about it, do you?"

"What?"

"What happened out here."

"Come on."

"It's a good story."

"It's an old story."

"But it's a campfire story and look," she pointed, "a campfire."

"That's good bogflutter."

"You're being dismissive."

"Oh, not really, I just . . ."

"You're scared."

He initially opened his mouth to refute this, but was distracted by another sound that seemed to come from the woods behind him. It sounded very much like someone trying to whistle but not doing a very good job at it. He focused on the sound, but then it dwindled away completely until all he could hear was the occasional breeze. "That was a long-ass time ago."

"Not that long ago."

"Eighteen or nineteen years is a pretty long fucking time."

"It was seventeen years ago to be exact, and you really don't want me to talk about it because you're afraid you'll get freaked out. Come on."

He let loose a big, exasperated sigh. "Some kids died, so what?"

"No, really," She scooted her blanket closer to the fire and worked on loosening her tawny braids. "I'm the local. You're not from around here, so it's my campfire duty to tell you. I'll promise not to scare you too much. I want you to enjoy yourself out here, right?"

"You won't scare me, it's just . . ."

"Okay."

"What?"

"Okay, I'll tell you. I'm a good storyteller. According to my nephew, I'm the best," she said.

"Your nephew is fucking eight. I really don't want to hear it. How about tomorrow night instead?"

"You're so scared." She wiggled her fingers into the loosened ropes of her hair, and it spilled out over her shoulders. "You're scared because you can feel something on this island too. You already said you felt a presence."

He squinted, remembering his words. "No, I said that the island has a presence. That's a big difference. Come on."

"Well, whatever you said, this place is haunted. The Chippewa, um, Ojibway, they thought it was haunted too. Not haunted by the sheeted and lost souls of some old white people, either, but haunted by spirits more primal. There are forces at work here that exist just beyond our senses. They don't care much about humans but—because their slightest movement dislodges so much energy—they affect us nonetheless. That's why this is such a sacred place. We get reminded where humanity ranks in the cosmic sense. We are infinitesimal. We should tread softly. We should spend our lives in perpetual fucking awe."

"And maybe you should lay off the bogflutter, sister."

"What?"

"That's crazy talk."

"What's so crazy about it?"

"Well, if we walked around every second of the day thinking of how insignificant we are on the scale of the universe, or even on the scale of the earth's history, then we'd be basket cases and we wouldn't get shit done. Just because you can conjure up these ideas doesn't make them real or productive to consider."

"I get it. You're scared. It's okay."

"No, I'm not scared. Here, let me tell you what happened out here and then we'll be done with it, okay? The way I understand it — correct me if I fuck it up now — but the way I personally understand the story is that there were these three college kids who got dropped off here to hike around for a long weekend, and some transient survivalist maniac came along and killed them. There's nothing too mystical about that." He held a finger up, signaling her to wait, took another long pull on his beer, and then stifled a belch before continuing. "It's not a good story. It's no better than some goddamn slasher movie. Crazy woodsy motherfucker comes along with his blood-splattered blades and hooks, finds their campground, and then slaughters them all, one by one, hunting them down like animals and punishing them for their unbridled teenage lust, right? Then the lunatic gets away and lies in wait for the next group of unwary campers who inevitably show up in the sequel."

"No, no, no."

"What?"

"Your account," she snickered, suddenly feeling very high, transfixed by the orange incandescence of burning bark curling near the edge of the fire. "Your account is both inaccurate and incomplete."

"No sequel?"

"The murderer was named Elliot Cook. He wasn't a transient."

"I remember his name."

"You want to hear the story or what?"

He braced himself. "I don't have any choice, do I?"

She smiled in the broken firelight and shook her head. "Not really. I won't take too long, and I promise I won't try to frighten you too much."

"I really don't scare that easy, okay? Seriously."

Her smile widened. "Okay. The story of the Great Hemlock Island murders. Here goes. Now, it was seventeen years ago this month when it all happened. As you know, this is a fairly large island with two of its own inland lakes. We are currently camped at the southern lake, Little Bear, which has its own small island out there where unhealthy amounts of mosquitoes reside. So that little dark hump of land you see rising out of the moonlit water directly behind you is an island on a lake on an island on another lake, okay?"

He rubbed his chin and nodded. "A lot of water around here."

"Indeed. Toss me a beer."

He complied and she continued. "So, this is Little Bear Lake, but the three campers who met such bloody misfortune all those summers ago were bivouacked at Big Bear, the northern lake. It's a little deeper, fed by several streams, and filled with yellow perch and rock bass. It's a seven-mile hike from here. We'll get up there tomorrow in time to fish for our dinner."

"Sounds good."

"But we'll have to camp up there somewhere. I mean, not too far from where it all happened."

"I know."

"You sure it won't bother you?"

"No, fuck—"

"It might bother you after you hear the whole story."

"Maybe. I won't know until I hear it, though, will I?"

"Okay." She took a big drink. "Well, like you said, there were three of them. They were college kids from way down in Prairie View, but one of them, Amanda Yew, had some relatives, an Aunt in particular, who lived up this way. She had been up around here—back on the mainland—several times when she was a little girl, and when she got older, she always made yearly plans to come back, see her Aunt, and hike around the island with some friends. She wasn't a novice. She knew probably every little bay and cove of this place by the time she made what turned out to be her final visit. And she was a pretty talented photographer. There's actually a book of her photography that was published just after she died.

It's kind of ghastly to look through it, though, because the last ten or twelve pages are filled with shots that were taken on that last camping trip. They were all shots of the trees. Capturing the beauty of the trees here was her primary photographic concern."

"There's some great trees up around here."

"Indeed, indeed. You're absolutely correct there, mister. This place gets most of its mystique from the fact that it has been miraculously spared from both lumbering and forest fires, and you can find some of the oldest trees in the region right here, especially as we head north. Lots of pine. Today we saw some younger stands of jack pine, but now we're camped in the moon shadow of two-hundred-year-old white pines, and tomorrow we'll see some stands of hemlock that have mind boggling longevity. Dendrochronology would confirm that some of those trees are four or five hundred years old."

"Dendrochronology?"

"The study of tree rings."

"Right."

"So, besides all the old pine trees, you can find

yellow birch that is a couple hundred years old too."

"Alright." He lifted his beer, drank, and once again and heard the sound of something whistling. This time it was clearer, but when he strained to pinpoint the location of its origins it faded away as before.

"So back to Amanda Yew. She was a very pretty girl, dainty and almost doll-like with these soft rounded and rosy features framed by springy chocolate curls, but she could build a fire and clean a fish as good as me. She loved the north country. She knew the woods. She convinced two college friends to come along with her. They were both men, Neil Bradley and Lazslow Peters. I think they actually spent a day or two in town, staying with her Aunt and getting acclimated, before they packed up their gear, registered at that ranger station back at Hemlock Point, and then were ferried over like us. The story goes that Neil and Lazslow had competitive romantic intentions with her, but that she was in largely oblivious to this. I don't know if you've seen the photographs, but both of the boys were good-looking in their way. Neil had been a jock in high school — a big and muscular young man, six foot three, two hundred pounds — while Lazslow was the somewhat chubby and more intellectual of the two. He lacked the muscles of his competitor, but he had brilliant blue eyes and a natural charm. Amanda had met him in a photography class. He was a Prairie View city boy."

"City boy?"

"Yeah, like you."

He grinned. "I guess I am."

"Oh, I know you are, but at least you're making an effort to evolve." She swatted away a mosquito buzzing near her eyes. "So there the three of them were. They had no reason to expect an encounter with anything worse than a black bear. They planned a five-day stay. It was July, but the weather was colder than normal and rainy. Highs during the day were in the 60s and nights were dropping down into the low 40s."

"Chilly."

She nodded, and then stretched her hands out towards the flames to warm them. "So, they set up camp and got situated. Only Amanda had any real experience camping in the northern woods, so she ran the show. She chose the gear and created the itinerary. They were dropped off at Miner's Point on the north side of the island and, as fate would have it, there was no one else out here during their stay. So after the boat that dropped them off sailed away, they were completely alone. The same inquisitive owls hooted at them and the same loons splashed in the waters and haunted the nightfall with their cries. Neil and Lazslow must've been pretty intimidated. Amanda knew the tales about the spirits that were supposed to grow restless come evening on these islands and, as evidenced by journal entries penned on previous visits, she had experienced some bizarre phenomenon herself. She wrote that she had heard strange whisperings coming from the trunk of a hemlock tree once, as if people were somehow trapped inside, and that she had also watched strange midnight swayings in the coniferous heights of those giant trees on windless nights. It is very likely that she told Neil and Lazslow these stories around the campfire at the end of their first day here. Amanda was fascinated by such things."

"So nothing happened the first day?"

"No. It was their second day when things started to go wrong, and it all began on their hike around the lake. They set off to check out an impressively dammed beaver pond. Amanda Yew, the wilderness expert and experienced hiker, twisted her foot on a slippery rock just an hour into the hike, causing a serious sprain to her right ankle. This, as you can imagine, was pretty upsetting to her. As the boys helped her back to camp, she was all tears and curses. Their trip was ruined. Neil and Lazslow couldn't wander too far on their own and the ranger wouldn't be back to pick them up for four days."

"So that's when the killer showed up?"

"Yes, that second crestfallen and discouraged night, sometime in the deep hours, Elliot Cook came paddling along in his canoe and they never even heard him."

"So they—" he paused, distracted again by the sound of a whistling coming from the trees. He thought of Amanda Yew hearing voices, imagined those faint whistles forming into words, and quickly tried to block the illusion from his mind. "So they all got killed that second night and that was the end of the story, eh?"

"No, actually only Amanda died that night. Elliot Cook did his work so quietly that the boys didn't know what had happened until she didn't answer the call to breakfast the next morning. When they unzipped her tent, they found a bloodbath."

He stared into the fire. The flames were retreating. The coals were shimmering orange. "Horrible."

She said yes, it was. "Her throat had been cut. Her hands were missing."

"Where did this Elliot Cook come from?"

"He was from Black Bay, a fishing village to the east. The place is quiet, and he was apparently always pretty quiet, too. One day he turned up missing. He just hopped in his canoe and never returned. There was no slow decline in his mental health and no criminal history, nothing leading up to what he did."

"There must've been something." He heard a much louder and closer gust of whistles and instinctively ducked. "What the hell is that?"

"What?"

"That fucking whistling!"

She listened and shook her head slowly. "I don't hear anything."

"Don't tell me you didn't just hear that?"

She narrowed her eyes. "Right."

"What?"

"You're fucking with me."

"No, I swear to God I'm not."

"You're serious?"

"Yeah."

She shifted uneasily. "Maybe we're too tired for scary stories. Maybe we should put the fire out and turn in. We've got a lot of walking to do tomorrow."

"You think I'm hearing things?"

She shrugged. "I just think the night out here plays tricks on people. I think it's the breeze and the shifting pine needles."

"Don't tell me you're the one who's scared now?"

"Sometimes being scared is the only appropriate reaction."

"Scared of what?"

"I told you I think this place is haunted." She stood up and nervously looked around. There were a few frogs calls and some tentative crickets, but otherwise the night was ominously still. "I think we should put this fire out and turn in. I think you might be hearing some of the spirits moving around and that's not good. Lazslow Peters heard the same kind of sounds the first night he was here, and they got louder the second night, after they found Amanda's body."

"Fuck off." He took one last drink of his beer, wincing the warmer suds down. "Don't tell me he actually found the time to write some journal entries before he got murdered."

"No, Lazslow survived. When Elliot Cook returned on the next night, the Prairie View boys were ready for him. A fight ensued. They had a single hunting knife and Neil, being the bigger of the two, agreed to let Lazslow have it. The story goes that Elliot Cook came back by water, apparently making no attempt to conceal his approach. They watched him from the trees as he slowly paddled up, landed, and stepped out, machete in hand. When he walked up to investigate the tents, it started to rain, and that's when Neil leapt out and tackled him. Unfortunately, Elliot killed him with a single swipe to the neck that nearly decapitated him, but Lazslow's attack was nearly simultaneous. All three of the men's bodies were crabbed together there in the rain and Lazslow stabbed Elliot Cook to death. So yeah, Lazslow survived."

"The whistling?"

"He wrote all about it during his years in the institution back downstate. After those bloody deaths he apparently unraveled completely. He cut the hands off Elliot Cook, mimicking what Elliot had done to Amanda, and then left in his canoe. They didn't find him until almost two weeks later. He said that he just kept paddling around the islands every night."

The sound rose in the distant conifers once again. "Don't you hear that?"

"No."

"It's getting closer."

She reduced her voice to a trembling whisper. "Let's put this fire out, okay, please."

He paused his paddling for a moment and rested the dripping oars on his knees, drifting ahead into the deeper lake waters on a tide that flowed strong and in his favor. The canoe drifted. His hunting knife was lying at his feet. It had not been cleaned. He saw a rising column of fire smoke winding into the starry sky, then lifted his oars by the badly worn grips and paddled on.

The Lakeplain Fiddler

Over one particularly hot summer, during the height of the lumbering boom, a grim woodworker named Timothy Fish built a new home for his family. This new home was a cabin located far from the sawmills of the town where he had been born and lived his entire life. It was no longer the type of place where he felt comfortable raising two daughters. They must be protected. Both of them possessed the same sandy-wheat straw hair of their mother and, in their fragile fashion, were unbearably lovely. Timothy dreaded this combination of comeliness and frailty. Being a devout man who regarded his faith as the source of his vigor, he believed their frailty came from a lack of sincere prayer—so he pressed rosary beads, lit candles, and beseeched the Virgin Mary to intercede and bring his family more firmly into the fold. His concentrated efforts in the matter amounted to little.

There was a third brothel now seeking discarded roses, and another tavern where whiskey splashed and swaying lumberjack songs roared forth. There was more fighting in the streets and even slippery murder by jack boot stomping. It was time to flee the town. It was time he took the necessary steps to shelter his women. So he scouted locations during the rainy springtime. He went far away from the town and far from the white pine forests, into a landscape more open. Scrubby little oaks were scattered about and the freshly green grasses below had the character of manicured estate lawns in spots. He could tell there was plenty of game. He also found the running stream known as Braden Creek, and heard a voice in his head that he deemed to be his lord. It told him your home will be among these trees. Your home will be among these trees.

So Timothy Fish labored hard from late May to late August, erecting a sturdy homestead for his family in a natural community known as a lakeplain oak opening. Such a place is characterized not just by low-growth trees, but by sandy earth and frequent blazes. It is essentially a fire-dependent savanna. Unfortunately, the woodworker failed to see this. He just knew it was close to Braden Creek where, generously dispersed in every direction, he could find serviceable wood. He would have to continue to make a living, after all, and would always remain a man reliant on auger, rasp and awl. He just no longer wanted to be reliant on that sinful lumber town. The women, on the contrary, did not share his concern, and brooded in silent disapproval of the move. Yet he insisted the lord had spoken to him, and therefore it must be so. So his daughters obediently went along with him. All three were going to miss the conveniences and opportunities provided by life in town: the stores, the theatres, the bustle of carriages, and the hum of conversation over unfolded morning newspapers. It was exciting. Now they were being pulled backward into the wilderness.

The daughters acknowledged they were to blame in the matter, at least as much as messages from the divine. Timothy had spied them one too many times, lingering on the clapboard walkways by the general store, flashing their lovely blonde smiles at sloping mill workers and shanty boys with rolled up flannel sleeves, bulging muscles, and bulging otherwise. The situation was becoming increasingly combustible. Emily and Lila had both begun menstruating. The men in town seemed to know, sniffing the air feverishly when they passed. They knew. They all knew. A change had occurred in the two most beautiful girls in town, and the more those disreputable workers pursued Emily and Lila, the harder and faster Timothy Fish labored on that cabin. He began asking them for more and more assistance during construction because he was becoming increasingly anxious when they were out of his sight. His wife Rachel did her best to keep an eye on them, but she herself was fending off new distractions— seemingly set off by her daughters' ascension into womanhood. Receiving and returning flirtatious glances with complete strangers was something she had never done before, but by the end of summer it was a daily occurrence. Once, in fact, Rachel nearly ran over her daughters when in blushing retreat from a recently widowed banker. They, in turn, had been in blushing retreat from men who could have been the banker's sons. It wasn't just those slavering lumberjacks and mill workers who were interested now. Maybe Timothy was right. All three women locked arms and strolled straight home.

Once their move to the cabin on the last bend of Braden Creek was complete in late August, it was clear that Emily and Lila did not want to be there. He kept himself busy, but the women, after things were unpacked and arranged to their liking, were restless and decided to explore the surrounding grassy openings one early September afternoon, skirts dragging across the dry bluestem and sedge — so dry and sandy that it occurred to all three of them that they were essentially promenading over a snapping tinderbox. The blue skies above showed no signs of rain, but it was not the pleasant stroll they had been hoping for. Grasshoppers sprang so aggressively through the air that they became horrified by the assault and sought a place with more shade. Just over a mile from the cabin, they found such a sanctuary where the land dipped into swales and the trees grew thick enough to offer unbroken shade and relief from the insects. There in the clustered shadows of the bur oak, swamp white oak, and pin oak, they could at last breathe the rigidity from their spines. An adequate distance from the stifling cabin of Timothy Fish had been reached, clear from the influence of his crosses and prayers.

But they soon discovered they were not alone because, after sitting in this tranquil spot for only a few moments, they heard him for the first time — the Lakeplain Fiddler. Rachel had been the first to detect his strange melody. She raised a finger to her daughters and bade them to be silent and listen. Emily and Lila trained their ears to the sound and whispered to one another in an attempt to name the lilting folk tune. It was to no avail. The three women followed the sound and found the musician seated in what was clearly a preferred fiddling spot at the base of a hundred-year-old tree. The upper branches stretched over fifty feet above, and the ground around its broad base felt wet. They knew this was a floodplain, likely to be under water after the thaws and rains of early spring. The fiddler himself looked moist — his slightly tattered coat actually dusted with moss, his beard curled into damp corkscrews, his exposed red forehead glistening with perspiration.

He smiled when he saw the three visitors and stopped his playing.

"So you must be the ladies who moved into that cabin over by the creek."

They all nodded.

"I imagine I am looking at a wife and two daughters."

They all nodded again.

He tapped his forehead with his bow. "And you came along because you liked the sound of my music."

"We came along," the young Emily cleared her throat. "We came along because it is unusual to hear music out of nowhere."

"But did you like it?"

"Your music?"

"Yes, my music. Did you like it?"

"I was trying to name the song."

"It is very old and very sad."

"Well, what is it?" Lila asked.

"It is of no consequence. If I told you the story behind the tune you would find it laughably sentimental."

"But lovely."

"Yes, lovely—but perhaps you would prefer something lively." The fiddler stood up. "I could play you a fine reel, the same one I play for the grasshoppers come September—if you feel like dancing."

Lila and her sister nodded but Rachel intervened. "That will not be necessary. We should be on our way."

The fiddler frowned. "I understand. But because you have graced me with your presence, I will leave you a token of my appreciation by this venerable oak tomorrow morning."

"What?" Rachel asked.

The fiddler stepped forward, locking eyes with Lila as he spoke. "I suppose it should be a gift of significance if I am to properly pay respect to the beauty before me."

Rachel swept between her daughters and pulled them close. "We are leaving now, sir. I am not sure a gift from you is required."

"Required or not, it will be here."

"And where do you live?"

"My home is among these trees. Your home will be among these trees as well."

And with that he was off, fiddling mischievously as he went.

The next morning, the mother and daughters found themselves in a quandary. They had not told Timothy about their encounter, fearing he would fly into a rage and forbid them any further wanderings. He simply would not understand. So they waited until he set off on his morning woodcutting duties, sour-faced and muttering something about his lord. The previous afternoon, while searching for wood, he had chanced across a dying elm tree with a heavy buzzing hive about thirty feet up. It was his intention to fell the tree and recover the honey once the stunned bees convened elsewhere. This would require patience, but he had to stay within sight of his prize and be vigilant should a bear hear the commotion and come to investigate. So Timothy would be gone awhile. The women were happy when he left because, once freed from the tyranny of his eavesdropping, they could revisit the topic of the

Lakeplain Fiddler and his promised gift.

"Should we go see?" Emily asked.

Lila nodded. "I think we should. We cannot properly judge the man until we see what he considers an appropriate gift to be."

"He may be a gentleman."

"He may, mother, he may."

Rachel thought about it, pacing over to the window and looking out at another arid and flammable day. "Oh, Lila, I did not like the way he looked at you. If we are heading back there to investigate, then I will bring the shotgun. Each of you conceal a knife."

"So we are going?"

"Yes, but not unprotected. Conceal a knife. Both of you! Make haste!"

The daughters obeyed, and the three women were on their way back to the dampish swale where that old pin oak stood. When they arrived, they found a feast had been left for them. Bowls of blueberries and nuts at the base of the tree, and on a green blanket was a freshly killed pheasant—the single arrow that took the bird still sticking from its plump side. There were also three loaves of bread and a bottle that they sniffed to discover was some type of fruity wine. They agreed that the fiddler had been quite generous.

"We should be able to carry this back to the cabin in one trip."

"But, mother, where is he?"

Rachel paced around the tree, scanning the oak openings beyond. "Apparently his graciousness extends to a choice not to be seen. Let's gather this all up quickly, with the exception of the wine. Your father would believe we produced all but the wine. It must stay here."

Emily picked up the bottle and examined it. "Are you sure this is wine?"

"I believe so. Now please cover it with some leaves and mark the spot so we'll have no difficulty finding it if needed."

"So we can come back and drink some?"

Rachel licked her lips. "If your father should go to town . . ."

"Can we try some now?"

Rachel leaned her shotgun up against the tree.

"Oh, I suppose so."

Timothy was troubled when his wife and daughters were gone when he came huffing home, nearly forty pounds of honey in tow. He set his satchels down with a thud. Not only were his women gone, but it was apparent nothing had gotten done around the cabin. They must have departed shortly after I did, the woodworker surmised, not expecting to be gone long. He looked for the shotgun, but it was nowhere to be found. Something was wrong. Something was definitely wrong. His anxiety was rising in a crescendo as he picked up his axe and set out to find them. On the first day of his search, he discovered nothing, and was forced to return back to the cabin with the setting of the sun. The cabin was dreary and empty without them. All night long the breezes hissed and kept him tossing, but at least some rain finally fell. The morning revealed a world more clearly in the grasp of autumn. Still, the women had not returned.

The woodworker ate some brook trout for breakfast and a slightly molded chunk of bread slathered with his newly acquired honey. Had they set off on foot and made it all the way back to town? His mind raced. Such a betrayal was inconceivable. They had surely just gotten lost. Or been taken. The second day of his search was also unsuccessful, and he had wandered so far that delirium overtook him on his laboring return back to the cabin. In this delirium, he was sure he heard the sound of a violin playing somewhere. He pushed home and prayed. He wept. Finally, he rested. On the third morning, he went out onto the porch and was shocked to find evidence of his wife and daughters under his boots — their mud-covered dresses. Timothy dropped to his knees, regarding this as clear evidence of their murders. What darkened the fabric was mud and maybe something else. He had just commenced praying some more tired old prayers when he looked up and saw them. They were not dead at all. They were naked out in the oak openings, giggling and prancing away from him.

The following evening turned even colder. Timothy Fish had fallen ill with stomach cramps and decided it would be wise not to leave the cabin until his body recovered. But when he did leave the cabin and when he did find his women, he would kill them. Outside in the darkness, a curious wind coursed through the trees, gently shaking more green from their leaves and giving them a new tarnish in the moonlight. Then, the woodworker heard the sound of that damn violin again, soaring over those windy rushes. He bent forward in prayer. But the music kept getting closer. Some nocturnal fiddler was playing in steady approach. Timothy picked up his axe, gripping his abdomen and wincing. He determined in an instant that this musician was connected to the degradation of his women, and tried getting on his feet to take position by the front door when a particularly vicious cramping heaved him forward and the axe clattered to the floorboards. The woodworker twisted his body awkwardly to avoid the upturned blade and landed on his shoulder, which made an awful popping sound. He rolled onto his back and groaned. By then, the progress of the fiddler had brought him to the porch, and there the playing stopped. Next came a rapping at the door—

at first tentative but then insistent. Timothy tried to reach over for the axe, but his dislocated shoulder prevented him from doing so. He realized he wasn't praying anymore. He realized he should be praying. Then the door pushed inward and a violin bow tested the air in the opening before the door was heaved in the rest of the way. There stood the Lakeplain Fiddler.

"My good man, you seem to be injured."

Timothy groaned. "Back to the flames with you!"

The fiddler shook his head. "I've always had a fondness for bonfires, but my home has never been in the flames. My home is among these trees. Your home will be among these trees as well. Do you mind if I borrow your axe?"

Whatever Comes Next

Anna finished stuffing the last of her things into the back of her station wagon and returned to the apartment building to wander the halls. She hoped to find someone to drink with. It's Halloween night, she reasoned, and one of the tenants is bound to be having some type of party. The halls were subdued, though, just the usual muffled sounds of television sets and mumbled voices you would hear on any evening. She randomly picked a door on the first floor and knocked. A skinny, exhausted looking young man answered, and his eyes rolled behind his glasses. He occupied the apartment directly below Anna's and, although they'd never actually spoken, he knew her well.

"Trick or treat," she said, and then laughed with a snort.

The young man narrowed his stare, not saying a word. Anna was an obvious drunk, even when she was sober. She draped a disobedient strand of her dirty brown hair behind her left ear and smiled. Her grin made the broken blood vessels that covered her nose seem to glow.

"How's it goin'?" she asked, trying to be friendly. "Are you the one who's havin' a party tonight?"

He shook his head, annoyed, and went to close the door, but she took a step forward. "Yeah, well, I knew someone on this floor was havin' some type of party and I thought this was the place. Guess I was wrong. You know where it is?"

"What?"

"The party."

"I don't think there's any party here tonight. Listen."

She stood still and listened. "Yeah, hey, it is real quiet, ain't it?"

He nodded. "Maybe it's upstairs."

"No, it ain't upstairs. I was just up there." She licked her teeth and coughed. "I'm all moved out. I'm leavin' tonight. I was hopin' someone was doin' somethin' tonight, ya know, my last night in town. It's Halloween! What's wrong with these people, huh?"

He shrugged and tried to shut the door again, but she put a hand out and stopped him. He looked down at her hand, breathing hot, disgusted air through his nostrils.

"Come on, let me in and we'll have a drink, huh?" she said.

He gently moved her hand away. "Number one, I don't like to drink, and number two, I don't even know you. I've heard you, believe me, I know what your voice sounds like comin' through the goddamn ceiling at about three o'clock in the morning but . . ."

"Anna?"

They both turned to look at the hulking man who was standing at the top of the stairs, removing his gloves. It was the landlord's cousin Jamie, who worked maintenance and also acted as the private policeman of all their rental properties. Anna felt her stomach clench up when he repeated her name.

"What's goin' on here, Anna?" he asked.

"Nothin', just talkin' to my friend here," she replied.

"Really? So, Matthew, Anna is your friend,

huh?"

The young man shook his head.

Jamie grinned with the smugness of a lifetime bully. "Would you mind if I talked to Anna alone?"

"Nope," the young man said quickly, shutting the door so fast that it nearly caught Anna's hand. Alone with Jamie in the dark hall, she was afraid. Anyone who lived in a place owned by Crane Properties long enough eventually heard a story or two about Jamie. Just a few months ago, someone had filed an erroneous complaint that one of the residents on the bottom floor was smoking crack in her room at night. Laura was the name of the accused and, truth be told, she had never smoked crack in her life. She was nothing more than a harmless and exceedingly boring run-of-the-mill pothead. Jamie, a physical fitness lunatic who despised substance abuse, paid her a surprise visit, found her stash, and then kept her in a headlock until the police arrived, even though she had apparently never made an attempt to get away. The docile and slightly bruised Laura was evicted, arrested, and never heard from again.

Anna took a step backward.

"What are you still doin' here, Anna?" Jamie asked.

"I was just leavin'. All my things are packed up and gone. Go on and see for yourself."

Jamie admired his right hand in the low light with pride. It was a gesture meant to intimidate her by drawing attention to his wide, scarred spread of knuckles. "You were supposed to be outta here three days ago, Anna."

"I know, I talked to Duane and he said it was alright if I took a little extra time because I haven't had any help and—"

"Duane didn't tell you shit. Duane wants you out of here. That's why he sent me." He turned to go back down the stairs and gestured for her to follow. "Come on, let's go."

Dejected, she descended the steps behind him. Once they were on the front porch, he slammed the front door and locked it. Anna stared at the secured entrance numbly, shocked by the realization that she'd probably never walk through it again. She had spent nearly two years of her life calling the address home, but now it was over. It was curious how a door that had always seemed so welcoming could quickly become nothing more than a barrier.

"Closed doors sure ain't real friendly," she said.

Jamie held out his hand. "I need your keys."

Anna could feel her bad tooth start to throb. She looked across the street and saw a group of trick-or-treaters swarming up the breezy sidewalk, costumes flapping in the kicked-up leaves. A couple of parents followed them at a discreet distance. Sure is nice to be a kid like that, she thought, with older people watchin' out for you and getting everything for free but shit, I'd never go through it again, not for all the tea in China. Those kids are happy because they don't know what's in store, she thought, guess that might be the only kind of real happiness there is.

"Anna, I need your keys."

She glared at Jamie. "Yeah, hold your horses."

He waited impatiently while she went digging through the mess in her purse. She came across an empty pack of cigarettes and moaned — looking up at Jamie with her best pleading eyes.

"You got a cigarette?"

"Don't smoke." He held out an empty palm. "The keys, Anna."

The trick-or-treaters had crossed the street and were passing by the apartment building. She went out to meet them.

"Hey, kids, any of you gotta cigarette?"

The parents were quick in coming to the rescue, pulling the children away from Anna with harsh whispers of reprimand and caution. She dimly realized that one of the protective mothers was about her own age. A heavy hand fell on her shoulder and she turned around to find Jamie breathing in her face. It was a cold night and his breath was coming out in clouds, blinding her.

"I ain't got all night, Anna, give me the fuckin' keys so I can get outta here." He ground his teeth together and his jawbone stood out. "Unlike most of the people around here, I actually have a life and things to do, and I'm already runnin' late."

"You're not very nice," said Anna.

"I don't care what you think. You've been a pain in the ass here for a long time. Why should I be nice to you, huh?"

"Because I'm a lady."

He laughed.

"I am a lady and you should at least be concerned with what's gonna happen to me." Her voice quivered. "You just kick me out of my place where I've lived for so long and throw me out in the street like this, and you don't even care what happens to me?"

"Nope, just give me the keys and quit bein' an asshole."

Anna continued to look in her purse while she talked. "I guess that at least I've still got my station wagon, and that's good because I can drive somewhere new, maybe head down South before it gets too cold up here, ya know? I could find some type of job down there. I've got cousins somewhere in Kentucky — Lexington, actually, that's horse country down there and it's real nice and I'm a damn good waitress, damn good. I'll find some other job. I just have to leave this town, that's all there is to it. This place is bad luck."

She found her keys and handed them over. Jamie inspected them and nodded. "You wanna know what

I think you should do? I think you should stop drinkin'."

Anna didn't know how to reply. Before she could find any words, he had walked off the porch and was down the sidewalk getting into his truck. She thought about running after him to tell him what a piece of human shit he truly was, but she remembered frail Laura in a headlock. She remembered the size of his shoulders and his hands, and decided that it was best to keep quiet. He aggressively revved up his monster engine and drove by without looking at her. She was invisible now.

"Someday, he'll pay for bein' such a cocksucker. He'll burn in hell," she said, and then remembered she no longer believed in hell. "Well, somethin' bad will happen to him. Somethin' bad happens to everybody sooner or later."

Another band of trick-or-treaters came up the block as she crossed the sidewalk. One of them was dressed as a werewolf. She'd always liked the idea of werewolves. It occurred to her that all of her old boyfriends bore some resemblance to her favorite monster. Michael and Phil both had unnaturally

161

hairy bodies and made almost identical doglike snarls and grunts during sex. Gary, although never loud in bed, would snap and growl whenever he got into a fight, which was often, and then there was Rick who—with his thick beard and wild eyes—was the most wolf-like of all.

She'd never met anyone who drank more whiskey than Rick. She looked at the four jagged scars on the back of her hand and remembered the night he smashed a bottle into the flesh there when she tried to reach for the television remote. He'd been very drunk at the time, and barely remembered it the next day. Shortly after that, he quit his job, left her an apologetic note, and vanished. Anna still missed him. It was hard to believe that six years had passed since then. The boy dressed as a werewolf came up the sidewalk with his friends, bags heavy with candy. She smiled at them, but none of the painted or masked faces returned her smile. They just moved past her and hurried around the corner to the next row of houses.

The street was empty now. A few jack-o'-lanterns flickered from windows and porches as she walked through the leaves to her station wagon. She opened the door, slid inside, and jammed her key into the ignition. The engine groaned with the first try, but didn't turn over.

"Come on, baby, warm up. I know it's cold."

She tried a second time with the same results. She tried pumping the gas, then she tried letting it sit, but nothing worked.

"Fuck!"

Anna stared out of the windshield at the strange moving shadows of the street, watching the sway of barren, black branches against a darkened sky. When the snow started, she thought she was seeing things. With tiny drifting white sparkles, it began slowly, but within minutes the air became filled with a dazzling wintry display. Anna rose from her car and leaned back to catch the snowflakes on her face. The melting flakes tickled her cheeks, transforming the dismal night into magic. She excitedly checked in her purse to find twenty-eight dollars and assorted change. It was originally intended to be gas money, but the car wouldn't start and to hell with it, she told herself, let's get a bottle and celebrate instead. She locked the car up with all her earthly possessions crammed inside and started to walk towards town. A few blocks shy of the liquor store, she ran into her friend Short Charlie who had just bought a few bottles himself. He wasn't exactly the wolfman, but he was alright.

"Happy Halloween there, Anna."

"Yeah, this is crazy, huh, this snow?"

"Sure, yeah, we better get used to it."

"Not me, I'm headin' South like them birds."

Charlie frowned. "When?" he asked.

"Tomorrow. I haven't been workin' these last coupla months and I just told my landlord to kiss my ass, so what the hell?"

"Yeah, what the hell. That's great!"

Anna felt her bad tooth start to throb again. "So, Charlie, where you goin' to drink?"

"Can't take it into the Y so I was just headed down over by the river there—Hunter Park, you know . . ."

"It's kinda cold."

"Whatcha gonna do? Like I said, better get used to it, right?"

164

"Right. Well, you need some company?"

"Yeah, fuck yeah! We'll make it like a date, huh?"

"Don't get carried away," said Anna.

"We'll make it like a going-away party."

"That's just what I was thinkin'."

The snow was swirling around Anna as she rushed up to the store and quickly bought a fifth of cheap vodka. The clerk who took her money saw Charlie hovering outside and eyed Anna suspiciously as he stuck the bottle in a bag and tonelessly wished her a good night. Then Short Charlie and Anna were heading off to the park through the strange snowfall, flickering and fading, talking wildly and laughing like excited children.

A Man from the North Country

Not terribly long ago, in the north woods, a boy was born untroubled on a misty late summer morning in a cabin on Chester Lake. His parents regarded his arrival as a miracle and, as an only child, he grew up the recipient of their full attention and adoration. They called him Seth. His father was an accomplished woodsman and great carpenter who eagerly began imparting his knowledge and skills to Seth at an early age. As a result, by the time he could walk, Seth was already helping build fires, pound nails, and catch fish from bluegill to walleye.

His rustic education didn't stop there. His mother, straw-haired and Finnish, had an unmatched knowledge of the landscape and all its inhabitants, from flower to fowl and from critter to tree. She would walk him around the lake and through the woods, teaching him. Some of this instruction was less than scientific. For instance, there was an old trembling aspen they called Herman, and a leaning

166

tamarack they called Edith. They kept to themselves. Seasons passed.

In the autumn, the hardwoods would ignite, and the paths would fill with acorns and leaves that dropped showy red from the sugar maples, bright yellow from the birch, and rusty orange from the beech. Cooler breezes rushed through those brittle leaves and made the lake surface sparkle with drowsy October sunlight. Before the trees were even done with their shivery disrobing, the first tentative flurries would arrive. Not long afterwards, the landscape would shed its color completely and harden for the long hibernation of winter. The snow fell and piled up. Smoke rose daily from the chimney of their little cabin, and Seth quickly learned to walk and hunt in snow shoes. His legs grew muscular and strong. Slowly, the energetic boy matured to become an impressive example of vigorous manhood. His jaw grew to resemble a granite outcropping in the process. One could imagine him becoming an inspiring leader, a great general perhaps, maybe even a famous athlete. Suffice it to say that Seth seemed destined to make an impact on the world if he could ever part from the northern wilderness he loved so well. It would be hard to go. What could compare to the unsurpassed beauty of a frozen Chester Lake glittering in the cold sunlight of a winter's dawn?

Winter was hard, of course, but it was his favorite time of the year. He loved the great silence of the season, and felt a special kinship with the animals that remained, especially the tiniest among them, like those resilient chickadees and tree sparrows that could always be seen hopping along on the hard snow. When the big thaw finally came, there they were on the slippery mud and exposed dead grass, still hopping along. They remained. They endured. Strong little birds. Slowly, the green returned for them and, summoned by this vernal rejuvenation, so did all other creatures on the wing. Those chickadees and sparrows were rejoined by swallows, flycatchers, meadowlarks and loons, and the forest filled with their calls and songs. The buzz of insects came back as well. Dragonflies darted over the lake and yellow jackets followed the drifting aroma of wildflowers that came blooming as the ground softened with the warmer rains. The rhythmic seasons passed in this manner, and Seth could hear the different winds speak to him. There was a strain of the mystic on his mother's side of the family that made his connection to the intangible particularly strong. Some people would say he had a fine intuition and leave it at that, but a fine intuition won't open you up to the cryptic language of the breezes, now will it? In another time he might've stayed in those woods and become a shaman, but this was the modern world, and his days on Chester Lake were numbered. Soon a wanderlust would take root in him that would carry him away to the city.

One day, in the October of his twentieth year, his wanderlust was born. He parked his pick-up next to a shiny black roadster outside the general store of Chester Lake. As the dust and dead leaves of his arrival settled, he stepped out of his truck, stretched his big flannel-clad muscles, and walked cautiously alongside the car, admiring the reflecting chrome and sleek design. He'd never seen anything like it. Moments later, the owner of the automobile came out of the store and lit a cigarette. He was wearing a black suit and a yellow shirt. Both his dark hair and thin moustache were neatly trimmed. Seth had never seen anything like him, either.

The man reacted to Seth's smile by narrowing his eyes and blowing a big cloud of smoke into the air. The door behind him opened again and a woman walked out, pressing the creases out of her black skirt. Sorry, honey, hadda use the bathroom, she said. Seth tried not to stare but couldn't help it. She had a wild mess of brunette hair, a strange way of talking, and a sexy red lipstick smile which she flashed in his direction. Seth tried to smile back but could tell that his face muscles weren't complying. The man put an arm around the woman's little waist and guided her into the passenger's seat, then gave Seth a mean stare before climbing in himself and driving off. Seth watched until the car had rolled out of sight and up the road, heading with dangerous speed in the direction of the highway.

Inside, he talked to the man behind the counter, an older local named Beauchamp, and found out that the couple was from the city and they'd come in for directions. They were lost, he said, why else would someone come through here, right? If you ain't planning on hunting or hiking, then there's no good reason to traipse up this way. Those folks sure as heck weren't planning on hunting or hiking. Seth listened to all this while scratching that granite chin of his and, well, that was the exact moment he started to consider investigating this big city on his own.

In the weeks that followed, Seth would sometimes linger in town just hoping that the same roadster, minus the fancy gentleman, would cruise in and maybe need some help. It didn't happen but, as could be expected, the big city brunette began making regular appearances in his dreams. He imagined that he was the man in the suit, and that it was his arm wrapped around her waist. He wondered what those red lips might taste like. Cherries? He loved cherries. Apples? He loved apples, too. Trying to imagine what her flavor might be was driving him to distraction, and it fed an ever-increasing desire to get the hell away from Chester Lake.

One day after chopping wood in December, he decided to tell his parents he was leaving. He told them he would only be gone for a while, would write letters to keep in touch, and would return with a windfall of money by the following yuletide. He told his parents that he was a young man, and this was the time in his life when he could start making a real contribution.

"You've worked for me these years," he told them, "supporting me, educating me, and it's only fair that I do some work for the two of you now. We could use the extra money and the city is loaded with it. It's there for the taking. That's where I'm going." This, of course, broke their hearts, but they believed in their son and had faith that a small sampling of city life would be enough to satisfy his curiosity and send him home. So, just after Christmas and with much embracing and weeping, they wished him the best and off he went. Along the way, he said farewell to Herman, the trembling aspen, and Edith, the leaning tamarack. With a single suitcase of clothes and several pairs of boots tossed in his flatbed, he crunched down the icy dirt road that ran with the switchgrass to the highway and was gone.

Where there were once natives in furs and braids stepping lightly around crackling nocturnal fire pits while wolves howled from the primal depths of the ancient woods, there were now wide avenues that quavered with a pulsating frenzy of impatient automobiles. Bright lights flashed. Music blared. People shouted at one another to be heard. It was the big city — the City of Riverbend. Seth had done a little reading about the history of his destination, courtesy of the Chester Lake Public Library in order to prepare himself. So he knew that the old wetlands had been drained long ago. He also knew that first there were farms, then came the booming shipyards and then, with belching black clouds and smokestacks, came further and more imposing varieties of industry.

The wolves, near the beginning of this process, had been shot at with rifles and had run off. The denigrated natives shamefully received the same general ill-treatment. Things had been relatively peaceful for thousands of years, but things changed fast. The old-growth forests were soon completely gone, while in their place a densely packed contagion of humanity began to spread. Consequently, the construction to accommodate all these new bodies was perpetual. The increasingly urban race to keep up with the demands of all these migrants and immigrants had a tangible intensity that buzzed and popped like a thousand combustible engines. The City of Riverbend—it had sprouted from a fur-trading outpost into a sprawling jag of concrete and steel in a mere two hundred fifty-nine years.

Seth spent the first few days walking around slack-jawed and wide-eyed. Imagine the comic representation of an adult hayseed in his initial encounter with the cosmopolitan. That was him. But soon he gained some equilibrium and composure. He was a capable young man, after all. Before leaving Chester Lake, he had spent long hours with his father getting some final advanced lessons in carpentry. These carpentry skills, combined with his physical strength and stamina, helped Seth find steady work shortly after his arrival. It made him happy. He would earn a paycheck by building things with his hands which, in this new frantic environment, was one of the few honest jobs that paid well. Sure, the work could be repetitive, but it wasn't so bad and

Seth was good at it. The men who worked alongside him were amazed that he could toil for such long hours without taking a single break and that, at the day's end, he seemed as fresh and robust as ever. New guy, they called him.

They were equally impressed with his tolerance for the cold, especially his fellow workers who had moved up from more tropical climates to the South. Those men piled on layers and coats because they found the freezing weather to be unbearable, but Seth would often show up for work on snowy days hatless, coatless and happily whistling bird calls with his head full of chickadees and sparrows. He was predictably asked where he hailed from and Seth, determined to protect the sanctity of Chester Lake, made only vague references to mountains far away in the west where wooden crosses marked the graves of the last of his relatives. Many of the men who came to the city alone had such stories, some more obvious in their falsity than others, and they were always greeted with understanding nods. No one was willing to begrudge a fellow wayfarer the chance at a fresh start. The past was the past. Let it lie.

Seth forged a friendship with one of these shivering Southerners in particular, a man named George, who had drifted to the city with his sister. They lived in the same dirty neighborhood. Factory smoke obscured the night sky. The refuse of the distracted and the defeated carelessly littered the streets. Seth paid a meager rent to live in a tall building next to another tall building that unfortunately kept all direct sunlight from his window. People who live with concrete between their feet and the earth lose a vital connection, George told him, that's why I keep my memories of home secure in my heart. I don't want to forget the feeling of that dirt under my feet. Seth agreed with George and became increasingly troubled by the gradual deprivation of his own senses. His inner mystic dimmed. Even his golden hair was getting drained of its shine. George convinced him that whiskey, especially in the cold months, would improve his mood and for a while. The whisky helped, but soon— no matter how many bottles he emptied—the grime and noise started to make their inevitable and democratizing marks.

The vibrant outlook that once set him apart from his fellow workers had been slowly worn away in a matter of a few cold months. His eyes dimmed a bit and his shoulders stooped. He'd had enough. One night in late March, he walked out of the bar with George, found that his truck had been stolen, and proceeded to angrily kick at the slush and ice in frustration. "I want clean snow," he said, "I want my snowshoes and my goddamn woods back. I wanna see my Mom and Dad and Herman and Edith."

George placed a consoling hand on Seth's big shoulder and told him that things would be alright. "My sister Geraldine will come get us, he said, let me go back inside and give her a call." George called his sister Geraldine and, a few minutes later, she pulled up in a long, crazy car with fins. Seth hadn't met her up until that point, but the moment he saw her in those dashboard lights, singing along to the radio, he completely forgot about those snowshoes and those quiet woods.

Geraldine was three years younger than Seth, but they were nearly identical in height. Her smile was the brightest thing he'd seen since moving into the city and, in spite of everything, she smiled often. It made Seth feel rather weak, considering he'd almost let his spirit get broken by all the concrete and noise in so short a time while this amazing woman had seen and been through far worse while still maintaining a defiant cheerfulness. George seemed to immediately pick up on the electric connection between his sister and friend and, perhaps realizing it would be futile to interfere, offered to take the back seat so that Seth and Geraldine could ride together up front. They couldn't stop beaming at one another, and soon they were making phone calls and then making dates.

Spring arrived, love unfurled in its way, and their courtship proceeded. She worked at the downtown hospital as a student nurse, took night classes and, even after these taxing endeavors, still had what appeared to be an endless supply of energy for exploring. Seth learned that much of this energy came from the consumption of Benzedrine, which she gleefully purloined from her employer. She was just what Seth needed. She made him realize what a claustrophobic rut he'd been in. She shook him up. Before he met her, he was slipping into the habits of a man much older than himself. He worked. He went to the bar. He went home. He slept. Then he woke up and did it again. On weekends, he rarely strayed from his neighborhood. Geraldine, brazen spark-plug that she was, changed all that. She drove him all over the city in her crazy car and showed him museums, parks, and restaurants he never knew existed. She introduced him to some musician friends, and he started smoking filter-less cigarettes. She helped him pick out a couple flattering neck-ties. She took him to sweaty nightclubs. She introduced him to gin and reefer. She made him laugh and gave him delicate instruction in the ways of lovemaking. Touch me like this, she demonstrated. Seth was learning. He was finally beginning to understand the rewards of living in the big city.

He was falling, for the first time, in love. Geraldine became the only person he met in Riverbend who learned the truth about his origins on Chester Lake. He made her swear to secrecy. He silently couldn't help but imagine some tranquil future for the two of them in those northern woods. "Maybe in the summer we can drive up there," she said, "we'll just sneak away one night, I'd love to see it." He kissed her and she kissed back, and they were together almost every night. She stayed in his apartment and their long naked bodies rested entwined, side by side, floating, cockroaches skittering in the darkness around them. In the mornings he would rise early, and she would rise early with him to drink coffee and listen to the news on the radio.

Soon the winter ice started to break up and melt down the sidewalks. The buildings dripped, windows were opened, and stale air was released. You could smell people cooking, hear their voices, and hear their music. The long hibernation of the cold season ended, and potted flowers bloomed on balconies. Seth felt a rare happiness. Not only was he consumingly enamored with a wonderful woman, but he was slowly falling in love with the city, too. All day long while he worked, he thought about Geraldine and what they had planned to do next. He caught himself whistling jazz melodies instead of bird calls when he envisioned her sparkling brown eyes, that throaty laugh, and the panacea of her long-fingered hands that played so lightly on his sore muscles.

Then, one day in July, George was called away by the boss and when he returned, it was clear that something terrible had happened. There had been a car chase and an accident. Geraldine and a co-worker were walking along on their lunch break not far from the hospital when the chase came around the corner and the police car in pursuit lost control, flipped, and skidded into them on the sidewalk. Geraldine's friend lingered comatose for weeks, but young Geraldine had been killed instantly.

Summer returned, but its warmth provided little consolation to Seth. He was despondent. His grief kept him awake during the long, hot nights, sitting shirtless by his window with a borrowed fan plugged in and oscillating, dabbing away sweat and dabbing away tears. His inability to comprehend the tragedy of Geraldine's death resulted in a steady darkening of his outlook, especially after the crying stopped. He saw the world more and more as a cruel place. He wrote dark letters home to his parents which he always tore up before sending. I will explain when I emerge from the other side of this, he told himself, all they will do is worry if I report to them now. It's best to ride this out like a man.

Charles, equally distraught over the loss of his sister, invited Seth to join him in finding solace in church, but Seth wanted no part of it. He holed himself away. He brooded. He looked deep into himself for the answers. Remarkably, this grieving did not inspire a belief in the existence of cosmic evil. He concluded by bourbon one night that the forces at work in this world that influence our tiny lives are neither good nor evil. Everything is random. It's just the misguided human tendency to imbue every goddamn thing with meaning. When something awful happens, it's easy to see it as the workings of some devil, but there really is no rhyme or reason. There is no luck in the end. There is no reward for being chaste and kind. There are just hours upon hours and days upon days where anything can happen. Seth then upended his bottle and fell back in his chair.

Who could blame him for these bleak observations? He saw the most despicable men in the city every day leading lives of many rewards while his beloved Geraldine had been turned from the loveliest of women into a mangled mess of blood and bones due to nothing more than bad timing. She was simply gone for no reason, and the silence in Seth's heart was deafening. He called in sick and drank away the steamy hours until — after one too many work days missed — he officially lost his job. He decided that he would admit defeat, use up the small amount of cash he'd managed to save, and then just head back to Chester Lake in time for the arrival of autumn, minus the windfall he'd promised. Had all of this really happened to him in less than nine months? It was hard to process. Three days after he'd made his decision to surrender, while imbibing alone at the corner bar, he was confronted by a man who had apparently walked through the entrance solely to start a fight with someone. The man saw Seth slumped over his drink, shoved into him from behind, and then demanded an apology. Seth had been drinking but certainly wasn't drunk. He was only slumped in such a manner because Geraldine was on his mind. He turned slowly to look at the man who was speaking to him and saw that he was a stout, wide-shouldered chap who already had his fists balled up in the pose of a pugilist.

"You should watch where you're goin', pal," he told Seth, "I better hear you say you're sorry pretty soon or you'll be sweepin' your teeth off the floor." Before Seth could respond, his burly tormenter popped a left that hit him square on his big jaw and sent him tumbling clumsily off his stool and down to the floor. It was a cheap shot. Once on the floor, the man kicked Seth in an equally gutless manner and instructed him to get the hell up. Stunned, Seth felt the blood rushing to his face where he'd been hit and all of the rage and frustration that had been boiling in him came cascading out. He sprang to his feet and charged his attacker, lifting him off the floor in a bear hug and then slamming him into an empty table nearby that crumbled beneath their collected weight. With his right hand free, Seth balled up a fist and began delivering powerful, skin-splitting blows. The man was soon begging for a respite, so Seth stopped and stood up to look at his damaged knuckles. While inspecting them, he calmly returned to the bar, righted his stool, and resumed drinking the whiskey he'd been rudely forced to abandon. The bartender brought him some ice in a bar rag to put on his jaw and hand and, while Seth was applying this makeshift compress, the bleeding man crawled across the floor, drew his knife and stabbed our man from the north country in the back.

Seth swung around with a blow so powerful that his cowardly assailant was sent sprawling and knocked unconscious. With the knife still hanging out of his back, Seth grabbed the man by his collar, dragged him to the door, and tossed him outside. Jesus, pal, you need a doctor, the bartender said as he went for the phone, but a man in a handsome pinstripe suit with a red rose in the lapel who had been quietly drinking in the shadows came forward and told him that it wouldn't be necessary. He introduced himself to Seth as Woody the Wolf and said he would happily take such a fearless brawler to the best doctor in town and pick up the charges. The only caveat was that Seth must go to work for him. Seth, feeling warm blood filling up his shirt and not fully comprehending what the well-groomed man meant when he said work, graciously accepted the offer and its shady conditions.

After recovering from his knife wound, Seth learned a few things about Woody the Wolf. He had evolved from guttersnipe to devout criminal to become the leader of a small team of thirteen thugs who rather predictably called themselves the Wolf Men. After proving themselves in various neighborhood grudge matches that resulted in several funerals, they started to indirectly receive jobs from all three of the city's top crime bosses. Woody took the work seriously and demanded professionalism and ruthlessness from his boys in equal measure. They mainly collected money and doled out punishments, but their bloody reputation grew, and soon they were stripped of their maverick status and pressed into working for one family exclusively. Woody had embarked on what he was hoping would be a steady climb right to the top of the underworld, and along the way he was always scouting for another strong arm that might hasten this ascent.

He saw great promise in Seth. "Have you ever made five hundred dollars for less than an hour's worth of work?" Woody asked him. Seth shook his head no. "Well, I've got a job for you if you want it." Seth asked for the details, and Woody told him that there was an ex-boxer with a gambling problem who owed his boss thousands of dollars and refused to pay up. "The guy is a real scumbag and none of my boys want to deal with him. Just go over to his place and leave him with a broken arm or two." Seth agreed.

The next night, Seth visited the apartment of the ex-boxer and was a little troubled to find a man older than his father standing there, shirtless, with a military crewcut and poorly rendered tattoos, holding a large cooking knife. Without provocation he jabbed at Seth, but Seth dodged the blade and grabbed him by the wrist in an attempt to wrestle the weapon away. The two of them tumbled back into the apartment and, after the knife fell to the floor, they began exchanging blows. The old man was a seasoned brawler and Seth pounded on him until his wrists were sore. It was like hitting a fucking anvil. They wrestled and boxed for ten long minutes until they were both cut and bleeding, and then they parted to slowly circle one another, panting, preparing for the next round. Breaking this man's arms was not going to be easy.

They continued to circle, and then the old man suddenly dove for the knife which, in their struggles, had been kicked all over the floor and was currently resting next to a lampstand. Seth dove for the knife as well, grabbing it first. The ex-boxer punched him hard in the face and, furious with pain, Seth retaliated with the blade and put a red gash through the tiger tattoo on his neck. The ex-boxer grabbed his throat and fell back, blood squirting between his fingers and spraying all over the floor. Seth stabbed him an additional seventeen times, broke both of his arms as he was instructed, and left the bloody apartment in a daze. He took the knife with him. The next day, he received a call from Woody the Wolf.

"You are a goddamn maniac," he said, "just the

kind of goddamn maniac I need." And that's how Seth became the fourteenth Wolf Man.

In the following weeks he made a considerable amount of money, always in cash, paid directly from the cleverly concealed safe in the basement of the hideout. His role was to be the knuckle-cracking intimidator and, every so often and only when called upon, a physical punisher as well. It really wasn't hard work. Unlike his first job with the old boxer, which he afterwards found out was a test, some of the other Wolf Men were always there with him, which guaranteed that those he hurt were severely limited in their ability to retaliate. He twisted a few arms, punched a few guts and faces, but mostly he just had to stand there and look as menacing as possible. He was given a shotgun and a handgun and, on top of that, purchased several different kinds of knives, including a machete, on his own. He bought a new suit. He smoked a pack a day. He wore black gloves to protect his knuckles. He stopped writing to his parents.

Autumn arrived and the city trees dropped their

colorful leaves on the pavement while citizens strolled along, their frames suddenly bulky with the new protection of heavier coats. Children were back in school, pumpkins and cider showed up at the market, and weekend radios blared football games, but every so often Seth felt a chill that seemed deeper than the one carried by the wind. It's just a job, he told himself, and soon we'll be heading back home. But his new violent lifestyle had the unwelcome effect of reawakening his formerly sublimated mystic. The ex-boxer with his gaping tiger tattoo began paying him ominous late-night visits, at first just drifting through the wall and then soundlessly out the door, but after a while the apparition began speaking to him directly.

"Get outta this stinkin' burg while you can, nature boy," said the corpse face with a smile of chipped teeth and rotted gums, "Woody's safe ain't all that strong and it ain't that well-hidden neither, it's right there in the basement of the hideout, slid into the wall behind that old busted up furnace. Easy pickings for you, pal. Sure, he's always got at least two of you boys down there guardin' it, but sometimes one of them boys is you, and you against any of them other chumps is pretty good odds the way I see it. Sure, it means at least one more killin', but then you can take a powder for good up there with the birds and the bees where they'll never find you and where you sure as hell won't see me no more. That's what you want? Right? Well, the way out is right there in front of ya, nature boy, easy goddamn pickings."

Sometimes he only talked for a minute or two, but there were other times when he would rest his blood-caked and singed fedora down on the kitchen table and fall off into long reminiscences about his boxing career that never seemed to end. Seth felt his mind slipping. He tried to block the boxer out, but the supernatural floodgates had been opened and, to make matters worse, even more ghosts started to crowd him as the calendar inched closer to Halloween. They were the ghosts of people who had died unnaturally in the building before. There were the two fat sisters, poisoned together, who manifested themselves to bicker in the echoes of the stair well, and the skinny lupine blue junky girl who liked to hide in the closet. At first, he tried to reason that they were just hallucinatory manifestations of his guilt over the killing and the beatings, but soon he knew better. Geraldine came to see him. It was the only time a ghost ever made him scream and cry. He knew that he would lose his mind if he stayed in Riverbend any longer. If I'm open to all the lost spirits in this horrible place then I won't last long, he told himself, maybe the boxer is right, maybe it is easy pickings. So, in desperation and with shaking hands, he put a pencil to paper and commenced plotting his escape plan.

It didn't happen right away. Things had to be done in an exacting fashion, and Seth called upon patience to be his ally. He discretely contacted his still-grieving friend George the Southerner, arranged for the purchase of an older model charcoal grey sedan through George, and then, without ever seeing the automobile himself, had it parked two blocks off the bus line on the west side of town on the day before he was to leave. He did not tell George that he'd been visited by Geraldine. All he said was that he had to leave the city quietly, no questions asked. George understood. George, for other reasons, had the same general ambition. They said their goodbyes, shaking gloved hands while wispy lake flurries fell on the avenue. It was the first of December.

"Last year around this time I was making plans to come to the City of Riverbend and now I'm making plans to leave it forever behind," Seth reflected, "but at least I'll be getting out of here alive." He said this last sentence, truth be told, in a very deliberate attempt to boost his optimism. He was worried. He knew it wasn't going to be easy—certainly not as easy as the dead boxer had claimed—but he concentrated hard and made every attempt to plan carefully. Now that he had the escape car all gassed up and waiting, the only other tools he needed for his liberation were a sledgehammer, two fully loaded forty-five caliber handguns, the knife he had taken from the boxer's apartment, and a sturdy bag with a drawstring. He had them all. He was ready.

The night after he had the sedan positioned, he was left alone with another Wolf Man, Hoosier Pete, to guard the basement of the hideout while the other boys rolled their way over to a local club. Seth liked Hoosier Pete. He didn't want to hurt him. This led to procrastination. They sat there smoking cigarettes and talking about Christmas for over an hour before Seth finally made his move. "I'm sorry, Pete," he said as he placed his freshly lit smoke into the table ashtray and stood up, "but I've got no choice." He then moved with such fluid swiftness that he met with no real resistance. He leapt forward, grappled his way behind Pete, wedged his way under his arms, planted his big hands on the back of his head, and locked him up for a headfirst dive into the concrete floor but Seth, in his excitement, used too much force in the takedown which resulted in a wincing skull-shattering crack followed by a slow pooling of dark-red blood. Hoosier Pete was dead. Seth scrambled away from the body, picked up his smoking cigarette from the ashtray, and went quickly into the alley where he'd stashed the sledgehammer and bag. He returned with these items to find Pete's legs twitching uncontrollably but, in a matter of moments, Pete fell still for good.

Seth slipped behind the furnace, removed the section of fake wall, and hefted the hammer onto his shoulder before swinging hard. The cheap dial cracked and flew off. He swung again, harder. Sparks flew. He kept up a steady clanking assault on the box until finally the door popped open to reveal ragged stacks of unmarked cash. He filled the bag, picked up the hammer, and turned to go when he heard the voices approaching. There were four different voices as far as he could tell. One of them belonged to Woody. The others belonged to Delbanco, Knuckles, and Boo, all Wolf Men. Seth was cornered. He set the bag of money and the sledgehammer down calmly, hefted one of his guns into his right hand, and positioned himself in the shadows at the bottom of the stairs. He'd see the first two sets of legs before they ever saw him. That would give him an advantage.

Delbanco's shiny wingtips came into view first, followed by an identical pair worn by Boo. Once they were visible up to the waist, he fired off two quick shots. One ripped through Delbanco's manhood and the other shattered Boo's right kneecap. Both bodies came tumbling down the stairs where they landed painfully, moaning, screaming, bleeding. There were no sounds from outside. Knuckles and Woody are probably quietly positioning themselves for battle, Seth thought, or maybe Woody sent Knuckles back to the club to get the rest of the boys. Either way, I have to act fast. He grabbed the blubbering Delbanco by the shirt collar and dragged him over to where Pete was lying face down. He took out his hunting knife, pulled his head back with a grab of greasy pomaded hair, and sliced open his throat. Delbanco fell in a heap, neck spouting.

Boo had stopped screaming and was watching with a strange, mouth-gaping disbelief. He looked up at Seth with glazed, traumatized eyes. Poor Boo. Just a kid, really. Too stupid to ever do anything but take orders. Finally, he broke out of his trance, wet his lips, and began speaking. It seemed as if he was trying to say hello to Seth when his neck was splayed open by the same blade that had dispatched both Delbanco and the pugilist before. Seth then heaped all the bodies together, grabbed the bag of money, and went boldly up the stairs. The door to the alley outside was hanging open. He walked through it and looked around. Snow was falling quietly. There was no one in sight. He stepped into the alley and an errant shot flashed from a rusty trio of garbage bins. Seth saw ghosts swirling in the air with the falling snow. He felt his own spirit aching to join them as he ran screaming towards those garbage bins, firearm blasting until every chamber was empty. Woody was alone behind those bins and only managed to fire off two wild shots before Seth was on him, gun tossed aside, and bloody knife drawn.

Beauchamp was idly counting the coins in the cash register early one morning when Seth came walking up carrying a single suitcase and a bulging drawstring sack. He was wearing the same exact clothes he had been wearing when he left almost a year ago, but was now without his truck. It was stolen, Seth explained when Beauchamp asked about it, that city is full of bad people and that's why I'm back. He bought a pack of cigarettes and then walked the rest of the way to the cabin where his parents lived. He never told them how he came across the money. He never went back to the city. His body slowly regained the rhythms of the seasons and the trees spoke to him again. The chickadees and sparrows hopped along on the snow. Chester Lake froze. He drilled a hole in the ice and dropped a fishing line into it. He caught dinner. He watched the moon rise.

Drunk Angel with Eight Arms

Denise stared at the tiny manger set up in the front room of the party. Everyone else was mingling in the back of the big house and she was all alone. I'm drunk on Christmas Eve, she thought sadly as she looked down upon the tiny figures. They all blurred and became animated. Stoic Joseph swayed and smiled behind a shivering Mary, and the crib that held the baby Jesus rocked back and forth. Denise knew her drunken eyes were playing tricks on her, but she was fascinated by the illusion and let her imagination flex to allow the display to continue. The little carved wooden wise men were comparing the gifts they had brought, bickering and boasting with their eager little eyes that each was better and more appropriate than the others. One of the wise men, the black one, delivered a kick to the one carrying the gold and he almost dropped it. The black wise man snickered and the donkey in the far rear corner of the manger crapped loudly into the straw. Denise felt her sadness melt away and she smiled a sinister little smile, taking another sip of her cocktail. The shepherds were all loaded on pasture wine and were barely holding themselves up on their walking sticks. One of them kept burping lightly and gasping for air. Denise watched him intently, sure that he was going to hurl at any moment. There was a roaring wind that rattled the glass of the windows, and that's when Denise noticed the tiny angel that was hovering on a string above the whole nativity scene. She bent down to look at it more closely and saw that the miniature cherub had fangs and was gnashing them together. Denise snarled, ripped the angel off its string, and threw it across the room. It must've forgot that it had wings because it just hit the hard floor and cracked in two.

"Well," she said to herself. "That was fun, but let's get back to the party now. I've gotta find that priest."

She wandered down the hall towards the tinkling glasses and loud voices, using the wall for guidance. She stopped when she came to a mirror.

"Hello, Denise, you crazy bitch," she said.

She used a swizzle stick to stir her martini, and then took a sip while looking at her reflection. What she saw there frustrated her to clenched fists and anger. There were dark crescents under her eyes from weeks without much sleep, and her make-up barely concealed the stress-related acne that dotted her forehead. Everything about her appearance was evidence that she'd been navigating her life into shambles. The white flapper dress she was wearing, which usually complimented her slender figure, was marred by deep creases, and her hair was drooping in a lopsided brunette tumble off of her head. Even her posture was ruined, fatigue arching her shoulders forward and causing her to slump when she walked as if she'd lose her balance completely at any moment and spill like dishes all over the carpet. People at the small party were taking note of her rattled condition, and murmurs of concern and gossip surfaced in hushed eruptions in every group she passed. For the early part of the evening, she'd catch their lingering gazes and continue along, pretending that everything was normal, but as the night progressed and one martini turned to four, she started to completely unravel. Her friend Penelope walked up to her with an unlit Pall Mall 100 in her red lips and grabbed Denise's clammy hand.

"Are you alright?" Penelope asked. "Why are you staring in the mirror like that?"

"I look like hell," Denise said bitterly. "I'm all dressed up and I look like hell."

Penelope let go of her hand, rubbed her shoulders, and spoke quietly in her ear. "Honey, you're being too hard on yourself. You've been stressed out lately, that's all. Maybe you shouldn't even be here, you need some sleep. Do you want me to take you home?"

"Sleep?" Denise said wearily, taking another drink. "He won't let me sleep. As soon as I crawl into bed, he'll be all over me."

"You can come crash at my place," Penelope offered. "He won't bother you there, will he?"

Denise nodded grimly. "He'll find me no matter where I'm at. And even if he doesn't find me, I'll just lay there awake, afraid that he will. It's no use, I can't get away from him."

She teetered and Penelope steadied her. "Honey,

you've had too much to drink. Come on, let's go home."

"No, I'm having too much fun."

"You don't look like you're having fun."

"Well, I am," she said sleepily, eyes wet and half-closed. "I'm having a ball, and I still need to talk to someone. It's important."

Denise pushed herself away from Penelope and weaved her way across the room to where two men were talking to one of the local Catholic priests, Father Holt. She watched as the handsome young priest followed his party jokes with witty remarks, and her hand tightened around her glass in boiling annoyance. The two men who were listening to Father Holt bellowed with laughter and glowed with smiles at everything he said but their faces went flat and blank when they saw Denise staring grimly at them. Father Holt turned his head to follow their gaze and grinned warmly, full of holiday cheer.

"Hello, Denise and Merry Christmas," he said, waving her over. "Come here and tell me how you've been."

You bet I will, she thought angrily, as she slinked

towards them, lips pursed.

"Me and the boys here were just discussing the most interesting thing. Did you hear about that young man, Billy something, who was in the paper today saying that he saw Jesus behind a strip club downtown?" The reverend forced a laugh and then playfully winked at her. "I was telling the boys here that being a man of the cloth, I just might have to go down there and check out the situation in person."

She kept her face expressionless to show him that she wasn't amused by his brand of humor, and this caught him a little off guard. He wiped the smile off his face and shifted his demeanor as effortlessly as a chameleon switches color. He placed two fingers to his cleft chin and hummed in thought. "It seems that something has been troubling you, Denise. I've been watching you tonight and you seem so distracted and glum. It's easy to get a little depressed around the holidays, I understand."

She shook her head. "No, Father, I really don't think you do."

He looked at the other two men and they read the message in his eyes, moving off into the party to leave Denise and the priest alone. Father Holt put a hand on her shoulder. "Whatever it is, feel free to tell me. If it's something that you don't want to talk about tonight, then you can always come to my rectory, no matter what time. I'm always ready to help anyone in the parish."

"I don't think that will be necessary, Father, but thanks," she said in a sarcastic monotone. "I just have one thing to ask you about, just one little thing. Last summer you talked about it a few times in church and you seem to be a bit of an expert on the whole phenomenon."

"What is it?" he asked, the concern in his voice strained even further. "Ask me anything."

"Well," she paused, as if trying to find the right words. "Well, do you really believe in guardian angels?"

"Of course I do," he said strongly, taking a deep breath and forcing his chest out. "That's one thing that I have no doubts about. Angels are all around us and I'm sure you're well aware that they're getting noticed more and more these days. It's because the world is becoming an increasingly troubled place that sorely needs faith in God. People need to know that God is with them all the time, and that's what guardian angels are for, to show everyone that God does care and that He never forgets about us."

Denise sputtered in laughter. "You really believe that shit?"

"Denise, I'm surprised at you. I think that maybe you've had too much to drink. I don't appreciate or deserve to be talked to in such a manner. I'm your priest, remember?"

"Yeah, that's right, you're my priest," she slurred. "I'm sorry, but I just don't think you know the whole story when it comes to guardian angels. Believe it or not, I'm a bit of an expert on them myself."

"Really," he said with an insulted huff, crossing his arms and cocking his head to one side. "Well, tell me more, I'm always open to new ideas on the subject. What do you know about angels?"

"Well," she said, staggering to look the priest in the eyes, "I know that not all of these angels are that nice, in fact, some of them are complete assholes."

"Denise!" Father Holt blurted as if he'd been

slapped. "I really don't want to—"

She held a hand up to silence him and then continued. "Assholes, assholes, assholes, some of them are real assholes. I'm speaking from personal experience here, Father. I tried to get in touch with my personal, special guardian angel just like you told me to in church last summer, and it was the biggest damn mistake that I ever made. My angel's name is Leo, and he's a fat, slobbering drunk who tries to get in my pants every chance he gets. Oh yeah, sure, he was pretty nice when he first started showing up and I was really amazed by the whole deal. Here was this angel appearing to me at night while I said my prayers, wings and all, incredible—I thought it was the great religious experience I'd waited my whole life for. Then he started showing his true colors, crawling into my bed while I was asleep, reeking of Wild Irish Rose, putting his hands all over me. I thought it was some kind of test of faith, but no, this slimeball was for real."

Penelope overheard from a few paces away what Denise was telling the priest and pounced over quickly to silence her. "Denise, honey, this isn't the time or place for this. Come on, let's go home . . . Now!"

Denise flapped her hand to dismiss her friend. "Please, I'm trying to tell Father about guardian angels."

Penelope gripped Denise by both arms and started to lead her away when the priest saw it fit to make a few final comments just loud enough so the other people in the room could hear. "You'll need to take care of your personal demons before you'll ever understand angels. I'll pray for you, Denise, I will pray very hard that you find peace."

He looked around, and was pleased to see that almost all the faces in the room were now turned towards Denise being dragged away by her embarrassed companion. Their two struggling bodies almost ran right into the Christmas tree that was by the archway leading out into the hall, grazing it and dislodging a few chiming silver ornaments. Penelope saw them fall but just kept going, wanting to be out of the room as soon as possible, out of everyone's sight.

Once in the hall, Penelope grabbed her drunk

friend by the shoulder straps of her dress and shook her. "What the hell do you think you're doing telling your crazy story to Father Holt of all people? That's just the kind of thing that'll get you locked up in the bughouse."

"Ah, who cares about that priest anyway," she said with an insolent jerk of her chin, "I think the creep was trying to pick me up. He invited me to his rectory, anytime I need anything, he said."

"Sure, Denise, everyone knows that he's slept with half the women at this party but that's not the point." She put both of her hands on Denise's cheeks and looked her steadily in the eyes. "You have to be careful who you tell this story to, honey. I believe you but I'm not sure anyone else will. It's better to keep to yourself, it'll cause too much pain if it gets out, understand?"

"But how can I keep it to myself?" she moaned. "This angel is for real and he's driving me crazy. Fine, whatever. I gave it my best shot. That lousy priest was my last chance for help and now I'm gonna do what I should've down a long time ago. I know that Leo will be here tonight—he can never resist the idea of me getting drunk without him — and when he shows up, I'll be ready for him."

Penelope didn't like the sound of that and asked Denise what she was planning to do. Denise just smiled, reached into her purse, and pulled out a shiny black .22 caliber pistol.

"What the fuck is wrong with you?" Penelope hissed, taking a step back and staring in open-mouthed horror at the gun. "Is that thing loaded?"

Denise nodded. "Yes, it is, and I'm gonna blow that drunk angel's brains out all over this party when he walks in. As far as I know, there ain't no laws against killing guardian angels, are there?"

"Don't be stupid, put that thing away, we're leaving." Penelope started to guide her down the hall towards the front door when a powerful gale of wind blew it open, knocking down a garland of holly and causing the dangling mistletoe to sway in the snowy breeze. That's when Denise saw her dreaded angel stumble in, bottle in hand. He was fat and unshaven, a cigar wedged into a wet lipped grin that widened when he saw his girl. He winked at Denise and came walking towards her down the hall.

"What?" Penelope asked. "What are you looking at?"

Denise couldn't answer. It didn't matter anyway; she knew what she had to do. As the angel passed her, she reached for the .22 in her purse and took a deep breath to summon the wild courage needed for the bloody act. Leo saw the gun and laughed, his big gut rumbling under his soiled, white robes. He went walking right past the two women, blowing Denise a sloppy whisker kiss. He swayed into the Christmas tree as well, knocking loose a few more shiny ornaments. Then he belched loudly. Everyone in the room had returned to their conversation circles and they just kept right on talking, expounding on all types of religious matters while a messenger from the Lord stumbled in their midst. Denise watched him and a burning rage began to swarm like angry wasps in her chest. Penelope grabbed for the gun, but Denise slapped her away and steadied a quick aim in Leo's direction. She lined up the shot in the middle of his fat head and pulled the trigger.

A deafening explosion shocked the party goers into instant silence. The bullet whistled straight at the angel, when suddenly he vanished and his bottle of Wild Irish Rose clanged to the party floor. The bullet continued on its determined trajectory through the open air where Leo had once stood and hit Father Holt right between the eyes, sending a wet splash of bloody brain tissue and skull fragments all over the white wall behind him.

The Mistletoe Girl

"Big Lou?"

"Derek."

"Big Lou. Holy shit. How long you been in town?"

"Long enough to feel fucking bored."

It was a crowded midnight just six days before Christmas, and Lou was wedging himself through tinsel laughs and jingle bell bellows up to the bar to order a drink. The stool next to Derek was empty, so he invited his old high school friend to sit. Lou said thanks and dropped his hulking frame down with a whistle. He looked around and merrily beamed. Decorations were everywhere—many of them as faded and tawdry as the place itself, but Lou loved it all. He loved the drunken loopings of multi-colored lights strung around the mirrors behind the bar and the miniature ceramic evergreen slowly rotating next to the beer taps. It blinked red and green and wet-snow blue. Lou felt home.

"So you're up in Salteaux now, right? Welldigger

Bay College?" asked Derek.

"Yes, sir. One full semester under my belt and they haven't kicked my ass out yet."

"An accomplishment."

"Hey, for me, it is," the big man took off his snowy cap and gave it a shake. "I'm twenty-four, man. If I'm ever gonna get my shit together it's gotta be now. I'm trying to take it seriously. How about you?"

"Working for my dad."

"Pipefitting?" Lou asked.

Derek nodded, close enough. "All-purpose plumbing."

"You're not still at home, are you?"

"No, I'm renting a place over on Vinewood."

"No shit?"

"No shit."

Derek finally caught the attention of the bartender and ordered two pints. "So really, how long you been in town?"

"Since yesterday," replied Lou.

"You should've let me know."

The bigger man shrugged. "Kind of a last-minute

214

thing. My folks decided they were heading down to Florida for Christmas. Figured I'd drive down to watch the house. They're gone until January 2nd."

"So what's the plan?" asked Derek.

"Find somebody to fuck as soon as possible."

"Same old Lou."

Lou shrugged again and felt his eyes drawn back to the front door. A crowd of bodies had exited and there was a new emptiness that allowed him a clear view of the young woman who entered. They saw each other right away. She had a petite frame and a long, waving gush of blonde hair that glistened with melting snow in the festive staccato of the window lights. Her pout was lavishly painted in freshly applied hooker red. When she let her mouth hang open to reveal the restless and glistening pink of an enticing tongue, Lou was mesmerized. The rest of the bar receded to a frosted nimbus fringe around her. He surmised the girl was likely not out of her teens and had no business being in a bar like this. She was dressed for a much more regal venue, and if not for her assured gaze and clear sense of purpose, he would have figured her for completely fucking lost.

Her gaze, in fact, was more than assured. She possessed the feral eagerness of someone raised by grey wolves. Her carnivorous smile seemed to say you, big Lou, are exactly the type of man I will consume tonight. In this fashion she kept her eyes locked on his, lingering in the doorway, then she pointed up. Mistletoe. Hanging directly above her. Lou mumbled something to his old friend and was off toward the doorway where she was waiting for him.

"You need a kiss?"

She nodded. "But pluck a berry before you kiss me. Always reach up and pluck a berry before you kiss me."

"I don't want to wreck the thing."

"Clumsy?"

"Maybe."

"Pluck a berry anyway. Just do the best you can."

The big man snickered and looked up at the berries on the mistletoe. "Yeah?"

"Yes, please."

So he reached up and twisted a berry off.

Immediately after the tongue-swirling mistletoe kiss they shared, the mysterious girl politely wiped the spit from her lips and hurried off, right back into the snowy night. Lou was left with his freshly ravished mouth gaping, locked in a stupefied paralysis while she made her escape. He could still smell the heavily applied peppermint perfume on his hands where they had clutched her scented hair. He could smell it long after he followed her outside, only to see those blonde tresses disappearing around the corner of the building and into the parking lot. The snow was falling heavier then, and the sidewalk was slippery. The big man nearly fell. She was gone. A luscious wisp had kissed him once and was gone.

The following day he thought of little else. He masturbated about her and then roamed restlessly around town, hoping their paths would cross. Fifty-dollars dropped over five hours at the same bar the following night was wasted. She never walked in. She never came back. You saw the way she looked, he brooded, obviously not frown Maquaqua and probably just out slumming for a kick and not coming back. Crestfallen Lou was one of the last to leave at closing time and found forward progress to be quite difficult on the huffing arctic walk home. The next morning he was cleaning vomit off the bathroom floor.

The following night he decided to save some money and just watch porn and drink at home. He needed to recover. So he walked the six blocks to the nearest party store to scan the beer case. The weather had turned oddly warm, almost forty-five degrees, and just after five o'clock, as the dull ashen hues of an overcast sunset faded and a starless night fell, a mysterious fog lifted from the melting snow. Everything was wet and dripping, and twinkling lights adorned nearly every house — casting a glow through the gathering mist, transforming what would have been a dismal stroll into something much more beguiling. At the store he picked out a case of Labatt's in cans and placed it on the counter. The rotund cashier met his smile with one of her own that was countless measures more robust and beaming. This woman is bursting with the Christmas spirit, he thought.

"You know that girl?" she asked him.

"What?"

"I said, do you know that girl? It sure looks like she knows you."

Lou turned and finally saw her again. She was in a blue dress this time and wearing a man's navy peacoat of the vintage variety. The coat was either the gesture of a gentleman moved by shivering feminine distress or the prize peeled off a bludgeoned victim lying face-down in a nearby snow bank; Lou couldn't tell. Her hair was piled on top of her head and she was smiling hungrily at him just as before. She pointed up and he saw it.

"Mistletoe," the cashier noisily chewed her gum.

"Mistletoe," Lou repeated drowsily.

Two more days passed without seeing the still nameless mistletoe blonde, and his obsession to find her burned even more fervently than before. What an embarrassment! Lou had inexplicably fainted after the last kiss and, when he awoke on the cold tiles of the party store floor with the rotund cashier gently shaking him, he looked around to find her gone.

Thankfully, the big man managed to collect his wits. He retrieved the damaged case, one busted can still hissing inside, and left on his own volition. But his collapse stung him hard. The next day he sulked at home and imbibed what was left of the whiskey, then what was left of his mother's gin. When everything on television made him depressed, he turned the damn thing off and fell asleep on the couch.

It was not a peaceful rest. The most dismal and murky dreams kept him tossing and, when the big man eventually did fall into deeper slumbers, he pissed all over himself. Of course he snored his way right through this indignity, and by the time he awoke the following afternoon, his urine-soaked pajamas were stuck cold against his legs and his teeth were chattering. Outside there was a fresh dusting of snow from what seemed to be a gathering storm. He really blew it with that pretty blonde. Out of your league anyway, he muttered. Thankfully, a text from Derek announcing a party across town that held the promise of easy women arrived at just the right time—the perfect distraction. Lou decided to pull himself together and go.

He got bundled up, with the long-suffering comic difficulty of the crapulent, and headed out. By the time he left it was snowing heavily, blowing off the frozen waterfront, the very direction he was heading. Along the way the houses got older and more interesting. The walk itself, in spite of going into the snow, wasn't so bad—just twenty minutes through familiar working-class neighborhoods with trees decorated and visible through the frosted blur of front windows. The walk wasn't so bad because most sidewalks had been cleared of snow prior to the storm but a few addresses, darkened by vacancy or infirmity, which remained neglected and treacherous. Around some of these forlorn places he thought he could hear the sound of bells ringing, and like all sounds when snow is falling heavy, there was a muffled distance to these chimes that prevented a listener from pinpointing their origin. He imagined these unseen bells gripped in skeleton hands and being waved morosely in slow motion to toll his passage. They were ghostly as fuck.

Lou hurried his pace. Soon a cluster of curbside cars and the low throbbing of music told him he had finally found the party he was looking for. There was the clatter of a storm door slamming and inebriated young women laughing that drew him in like a beacon fire. Lou bent his shoulders forward against the snow and forged ahead until he was saying hello to those same young women—both of whom were smoking now. They regarded him with casual annoyance, clearly unimpressed. He said whatever as he passed and went inside. Within a minute, he found the room at the back of the house where glorious alcohol waited, and there a tilted plastic cup under a tap held him in place. That's when he turned and saw her. This time she was wearing red, and her hair was wild from the gusty ravages of the blizzard outside. Lou had the strong impression she had been following him.

She pointed up.

Mistletoe again.

He drained his cup and dropped it on the floor. "What the fuck happened at the party store?"

"You collapsed and I left."

"You left."

"Yes, I left once the cashier came over."

"Guess you couldn't have been very concerned."

"Of course I was. I broke your fall."

Lou laughed. "Lucky I didn't crush you."

"Lucky."

"You ever gonna tell me your name?"

"Typhlobasia."

"What?"

"Just kidding."

"You ever gonna tell me your real name?"

"Perhaps. But first another kiss."

This time the kiss was more aggressive, and Lou moved his hips hungrily against her. The two fell into the doorframe. With his eyes closed, he had the sensation he was plunging through the doorframe and into a spinning whirlpool of confetti and fire. When their lips parted with a few last ravenous lappings, he kept his hands firmly planted on her shoulders—determined to stay on his feet and equally determined not to let her sneak away again.

"Well, I didn't pass out this time."

"Guess not."

"I've been thinking about you."

She tried to wiggle from his grasp, but he held

her fast. "No need to hold me so tightly" she said.

"I just don't want you running off. I've been thinking about you a lot."

"And no need to be so insistent."

"What the fuck is that supposed to mean?"

"I promise you will see me two more times before New Year's Eve—definitely before New Year's Eve."

Lou laughed and loosened his grip. "What?"

"You will see me two more times by New Year's Eve. I'm not going anywhere."

"Yeah?"

She nodded. "And let me tell you something."

"What?"

She leaned in to whisper in his ear.

"Oh, yeah?"

She nodded again and then, with the sudden agility of a chickadee, darted away once more and was gone through the crowd of bodies.

It was Christmas Eve, and Lou returned home with a freshly purchased case of beer and new sprig of mistletoe which he nailed above the kitchen doorway. He left the hammer on the counter and drained his first beer in three monstrous gulps. After belching loudly, almost as if in response to his belching loudly, he heard a slow creaking. The subzero night outside was still. He listened intently. In the far distance, Lou could hear the sound of a train barreling down the tracks—lowing and moaning, and somewhere a dog barking. Then, this time clearly from inside the house, a slow creaking again. He identified the sound as soft pressure being applied to the floorboards at the top of the basement stairs. The big man had tiptoed drunk as hell over that uneven floor numerous times and knew exactly what it sounded like when someone was trying to be extra quiet and tread softly. Then he heard another grating creak and knew damn well there was someone inside the house with him. He breathed heavily to rally his thinking. What to do? His father's gun safe was in the basement and not an option, so Lou grabbed a carving knife. The quiet footsteps were coming closer. Had he left a door unlocked? Why would he ever leave a fucking door unlocked? Too late now. Strange illumination brightened the otherwise unlit kitchen doorway, and then the Mistletoe Girl walked into it, wearing a string of throbbing red lights over a white velvet slip and nothing more.

"That's a nice long knife you have there," she said. Lou looked at the weapon in his hand. "Why don't you put it back where you found it."

He puffed out his chest and assumed what he believed to be necessary manly outrage. "How the hell did you get in here?"

"Down the chimney in a wisp of smoke."

"Really."

"Down the chimney in a wisp of smoke. It is Christmas Eve, after all."

At that moment Lou noticed a change in her appearance. Her complexion assumed a new moon-glow pallor—as if the blood was retreating from the surface capillaries of her face to pool in deeper veins. The transformation caused the big man to gasp, but those waiting lips were moist and he smelled the wetness lingering and beseeching from between her legs, so he balled up his fists and walked toward her with jaw-clenched determination. She was not getting away this time.

"You will see me once more," she told him. "Most certainly before New Year's Eve."

"Where?"

"Wherever you are, my dear."

Lou felt his breath quicken as he slid his hands back into her hair and swarmed in for another narcotic tasting, but it was clear to him that her hair was no longer fragranced by peppermint and his tongue was whirling around another tongue suddenly much colder than he remembered. He tried to suck the chill away, but the temperature drop continued until finally it felt like savoring a swollen bluegill. He pulled away and opened his eyes. Her skin was a deeper shade of indigo now, and a cadaver chill spilled over the big man as if he'd just opened a freezer. Then he looked down slowly, eyes widening in terror, at the plug from her glowing string of lights dragging uncoupled on the floor.

Lou took down the sprig of mistletoe from the kitchen doorway immediately after regaining his senses and brought it at arm's length out onto the icy back porch in the frigid darkness. There he set it on fire. When the last of the ashes fell away, he went back inside to make damn sure every door and window was securely locked. He was focused and efficient. Then he decided he would take his mother up on her suggestion to go to midnight mass, so he quickly dressed and made it there for the homily. The church was lit with hundreds of candles and obscured by billowing incense. It was warm. He took an apologetic spot in the last pew and those who heeded his late arrival saw a troubled individual— disheveled and reeking with a wildness in the eyes that suggested he had recently witnessed something unspeakable. His presence made everyone nervous. Especially after the sound of the pipe organ brought him back to some long-forgotten childhood recollection where he was standing in the same church at the hip of his mother—a memory that caused him to wail and break down in tears. The old man at his side placed a comforting arm on Lou's shoulders, but the consolation startled him and he shrugged it off violently, pushing out of the pew to flee back into the haunted night.

On the hurried way home, he spent the last of his money on vodka and beer. It was enough to keep him ferociously drunk all Christmas Day. In the morning he talked to his parents on the phone and told them nothing. He only remarked blandly on the amount of snow and how pretty the tree was decorated, and then hung up and responded to no more calls or messages for the rest of the day. By the afternoon of December 26th, he was sobering up and stir-crazy — a skyline of empty bottles on the kitchen table. The notion of cleaning it all up held little appeal. The big man was fucking thirsty and there wasn't a drop left in the house. He considered the bar where he first saw her. It was a place more hospitable than this empty house and besides, he reasoned, I'm not safe here anyway. Might as well be around other people. So once again he bundled up and went into the snow, back to the bar. This time the scene was dramatically different when he arrived. This time there was only one other drinker in the whole place — an old man in a bulky coat with ruddy cheeks and a sharp, Slavic nose. He was sitting at the bar, hand gripping a fifth of vodka, when he turned to look at

229

Lou.

"Come on over and have a seat. I'm buying."

Lou hesitated a moment. He had never seen the place so empty. Then, with a shiver, he realized why the old man was wearing a coat—there was no damn heat, his breath still pouring out in clouds.

"I said I'm buying."

"No heat?"

"They're working on the furnace right now. But, it's warmer than outside. Come on in and warm your bones with some poison."

Lou strolled over. "No bartender?"

"He gave me this bottle and left me in charge. Doesn't seem like a very wise decision on his part, eh?"

"Fuck no."

The old man smiled. "He'll be back in a minute or two. Trying to get that furnace up and running because there'll be lots of fellas pouring in here after dinner. You have a nice Christmas, young sir?"

Lou sat down. "Sure."

"Seem a little troubled. How young people can look so worn out is beyond me. Not getting enough sleep, I guess. Can't ever remember being tired when I was younger. You tired?"

"Sure." Lou carefully scanned the lightless smudges of the dimly lit ceiling and doorways. "You know if there's any mistletoe in here?"

"What? You afraid the Mistletoe Girl will getcha?"

Lou felt dizzy and put one hand on his forehead, the other firmly on the bar top.

"You really are afraid of her? You seen her?"

Lou shook his head no.

"You sure? She's not following you around?"

"No."

"I sure as hell don't want her coming in here again."

Lou opened his eyes and felt temporarily restored. "Shit."

"What's wrong with you?"

"Just feeling a little sick. Nothing contagious."

The old man seemed satisfied with this. "Well, reach around the bar there and get a glass. There's ice back there too. If you need it."

Lou did as instructed. "So who is she?"

"The Mistletoe Girl?"

"Yeah, who is she?"

The old man scratched the whiskers over his lip. "Just an old story."

"Like a ghost story?"

"Exactly, like a ghost story. She's been dead over a hundred years. Lived right here in Maquaqua and had family over on Wendake, folks with some money apparently. Some of them still live on the island, I guess. Used to go fishing with a fella who lived along the canal. He told me about it. Felton was the name. The Mistletoe Girl was Lucy Felton. Her family built one of them houses down on Van Alstyne—one of them old houses, ain't sure which one."

"Lucy Felton."

The old man nodded. "I know that for sure. The name of the Mistletoe Girl was Lucy Felton. Old folks say lots of things about her. Mostly the women are convinced she was really a prostitute. Seems pretty unlikely considering the money her family had. Lovely blonde girl like that is always gonna make other ladies jealous. So they cook up their stories and spread their lies. Women . . ."

Lou filled a glass with the offered whiskey, closed his eyes, and took a quick pull. Upon opening his eyes, he noticed something had changed in the old man. He now looked much younger and boasted a full moustache.

"She had planned a Christmas wedding. What kind of prostitute does that? And she was set to marry the dashing Avery Burrell. He was an entertainer on the Ashen Belle."

"The Ashen Belle?" Lou mouthed dreamily.

"The Ashen Belle—a pleasure steamer whose trim hull was launched right here in Maquaqua on December, 1899. By the following summer she was ready for service and ran mostly just up the river between Riverbend and Port Beyond. Avery Burrell strolled the decks playing his accordion for the people in those early days. That was where he met Lucy. The two of them were set to have a Christmas wedding."

"You said that—"

"But then came the tragedy of their wedding night. She went missing, never to be found again. Some say her bones are at the bottom of the river."

Lou felt his vertigo returning. "I have to go."

"But there is a bit more to tell. Don't you want to hear the part about the mistletoe? The baleful mistletoe? Look, there's some hanging in the doorway right now."

Lou spun around to see a scarlet glow forming by the entrance. With a long whine the front door slowly opened, corkscrews of snow looping in. The big man wearily stood up — the burden of one more kiss still upon him. When Lucy poked her head in, he noticed her once lustrous hair was clumped with filth and falling out. A tooth quivered and dropped from her blackening smile and a dark-green blemish of bacteria growth spread across her cheeks.

About the Author

Bob Stevens is a former party store manager, current librarian, and native Michigander. This is his first book in a planned series of thirteen.